The DEEP CUT

Susan Rosson Spain

Marshall Cavendish

Special thanks to Jason Grabill, noted Civil War expert, for checking the facts in this manuscript. Any remaining errors are my own.

This is a work of fiction. Though Culpeper is a real place and the Rossons a real family, for the benefit of the story the author has taken liberties with the town's geography and with characterizing ancestors, whose true personalities are lost to the past.

Library of Congress Cataloging-in-Publication Data
Spain, Susan Rosson.
The deep cut / by Susan Rosson Spain.-- 1st ed.
p. cm.
Summary: Considered "slow" by his father, Lonzo tries his best to help his family in Culpeper, Virginia, during the Civil War and, in the process, comes to some decisions about how to live his life.
ISBN-13: 978-0-7614-5316-1
ISBN-10: 0-7614-5316-4
1. Virginia--History--Civil War, 1861-1865--Juvenile fiction. [1. People with mental disabilities--Fiction. 2. Conduct of life--Fiction. 3. Fathers and sons--Fiction. 4. Virginia--History--Civil War, 1861-1865--Fiction. 5. United States--History--Civil War, 1861-1865--Fiction.] I. Title.
PZ7.S73188Dee 2006
[Fic]--dc22
2006001463

The text of this book is set in Goudy.
Book design by Patrice Sheridan

Printed in China

First Edition

2 4 6 5 3 1

 Marshall Cavendish

For my uncle,

John MacNair Rosson,

who provided inspiration

and endless encouragement

Acknowledgments

I would like to humbly thank the following people:

The members of my writers' groups, who read and commented on many first drafts and never complained: MARCIANS Lynne Brandon, Marnie Brooks, Laurie Calkhoven, Marcia Thornton Jones, Martha Peaslee Levine, Rebecca Kraft Rector, Mara Rockliff, and Barbara Underhill; Eastern Atlanta Literary Guild (EALG) members Stephanie Fenton, Sara Forbes, Sandy Lunt, Jay Sauls, and Greg Willits, Virginia Morton, for sharing her Custer research with me; and Writers in North Georgia (WINGs) Nancy Craddock, Connie Fleming, Maureen McDaniel, and Mary Ann Rodman. My editor, Margery Cuyler, for her expert guidance. My agent, Tracey Adams, whose response truly touched me. My first readers (who know who they are). And most of all, Randy Spain, who put up with my passion for writing and quietly endured the numerous inconveniences and indignities it imposed upon him; and, also, for being the best typo finder on the planet.

April 18, 1861

My lungs burned like hot coals in my chest and my legs was near to cramping, but I kept on running, fast as my bare feet would carry me. *Faster!*

The road ahead stretched out long and straight. I could see my house at the end now, the white fence out front and the big oak just startin' to leaf out. I dug my toes into the chill dirt for all I was worth. With Papa timing me, I *had* to hold out.

Pumping my arms hard, I near 'bout fell across the line I'd drawn in the dirt out front of the gate. I knew it was the fastest I ever ran in my whole thirteen and a half years and I grinned, proud.

But when I looked to Papa's rocker on the porch, all I saw was his legs sticking out underneath *The Culpeper Observer* and his big hands clutching its sides. A swirl of smoke rose up from behind the newspaper, lookin' like it might be his head on fire 'stead of a bowl of pipe tobacco.

"Papa—" I called out, bent over, hands on my shaky knees. My breath came in raggedy gulps. "Papa—did you time me?"

The screen door opened, and Mr. Stofer, who edited the *Observer* and was Culpeper's postmaster and telegraph operator, too, stepped out. Careful-like, he carried a steaming cup in one hand and his brown felt hat in the other. He blew at the cup. "'Morning, Lonzo," he called across the yard. "How are you, son?"

"I'm—"

"*Damned Yankees!*" Papa boomed, folding the newspaper in half and slapping it on his knee. "They're begging for out-and-out civil war, Alfred; just *begging*!" His pipe bobbed up and down between his clenched teeth as he talked.

"Papa, did you time me?" I called out again.

He bobbed his pipe some more, switching it side to side in his teeth and paying me no mind. No mind a'tall.

I picked up my boots from where I'd left 'em by the gate and started up the walk. Papa had stopped watching before I finished. I was not fast enough. Again.

Mr. Stofer waved his hat toward the paper before situating it atop his bald head. "You see where Lincoln's called for seventy-five thousand volunteers for Federal forces?"

"That's what I'm talking about," Papa said as Mr. Stofer settled into the rocker next to him. "You don't call for that many men unless you're serious about going to war. *Damned woodenheaded Yankees!*"

Mama called out from somewheres inside the house. "Keep a civil tongue, Bernard," she said.

Panting, I climbed the porch steps and stood in front of Papa's chair. He seemed to see me then, for the first time. "What is it, Lonzo?" he said, his eyes falling on the boots in my hand.

I wanted to ask him again: "Did you time me?" But it was clear he hadn't. There wasn't no "You're getting to be quite the athlete," like he said to my younger brother Will whenever *he* showed off. I glanced behind Papa to the doorway where Mama'd appeared, and remembering what she'd just said, asked, "What's that mean, 'civil'?"

Papa sighed, tapping the paper on his knee. Then he fixed them blue eyes on me.

I tried to keep from shrinking in my skin while he stared by listening to my little sister Mary Catherine sing soft through an upstairs window, and to baby Abner bang on a pot back in the kitchen.

"Your mother means 'talk nice,'" Papa said, quietlike.

Mama nodded and ran her hand gentle over her growing belly. When she moved back into the darkness of the house, I turned to Papa again.

"But Papa—that don't make no sense," I said.

Hadn't he just told Mr. Stofer the Yankees wanted a 'civil' war? "How can a war be nice when it's nothing but killing?"

Papa sighed, loud and long.

I chewed at a thumbnail, worrying the idea through my head. The thought of killing anything brought a crawly feeling to my stomach, same as when Papa taught me to hunt. I wasn't cut out for killing. I know men got to kill sometimes, such as rabbits and deer, for meat to eat. But you ain't got to kill a *man*.

Finally, Papa got up from the rocker. "Isn't it time you got on to school, Lonzo? And mind you put your shoes on. You'll get sick and spread it right through the house." He headed for the door, Mr. Stofer a step behind. "Don't mind Lonzo, Alfred," Papa said as he passed me by. "He's . . . well, he's a little slow."

I hung my head. Seemed like nothing I did pleased Papa. Mama said he loved me good—just as good as he loved my big sister, Emma, or my younger brothers Will and Tommy, or either of the little 'uns, Mary Catherine and Abner. But I'd thought if I ran faster, he'd love me more.

My cousin Ferdy called out as he came up to the gate. "C'mon, Lonzo, we got to hurry or we'll be late for school."

Ferdy was tall and brown-headed like me, but more'n a year older—almost fifteen—and skinnier. He slouched a mite under the weight of the poke sack slung over his shoulder, and carried a fat book. Ferdy nodded to Papa and his friend. "Morning, Uncle Bern, Mr. Stofer," he said, proper and respectful.

Mr. Stofer touched the brim of his hat and nodded back.

"Good morning, Ferdy," Papa said. "You're late this morning. Everything all right down at Winfrey?"

"Yes, sir, it is now," Ferdy said, closing the book but keeping his place with one finger. "Sadie busted the fence again. I had to find her 'fore I could milk her. Mama's tied her up out back of the inn for now 'cause she's tendin' to guests. I wanted to stay home and fix the fence, but Mama said I had to get to school."

Papa puffed on his pipe and a sweet-smelling cloud of smoke floated my way. "She's right, Ferdy. A man needs all the education he can get."

Ferdy stood taller. "I s'pose you're right, sir," he said.

I grabbed up my book sack as Papa went inside, and Ferdy and me headed out to the schoolhouse on Coleman Street. We had not gone a block when Ferdy opened up his big fat book and started to read.

Ferdy loved books near as much as he loved whittling and fishing. If he wasn't borrowing a book from our teacher, Miss Nelson, he was saving his pennies to visit the bookseller's room at the hotel. Ferdy read out loud to me and Aunt Mariah, and sometimes

Grandma and Grandpa, most every Sunday afternoon at Winfrey, which was the name of Aunt
Mariah's inn where they all lived.

I was not stupid, but I could never match the way
Ferdy read. I could near 'bout always puzzle out how
to say a word, but their meanings was hard to get a
hold of as ciphering or history lessons. Even when
the sounds came out of my mouth just right, inside
my head, the words might only be clouds.

Me and Ferdy walked along under the fresh-
leafed trees what shaded every yard we passed, Ferdy
with his head stuck down in his book. The air
through town smelled of breakfast: bacon and coffee
and biscuits, and all of it mixing up good with per-
fume off the brand new jonquils.

When we got to school and was all settled in
Miss Nelson's room, William Bowdry, the apprentice
at the newspaper office, stuck his head in the door.
He panted heavy, like he'd run the whole three
blocks, his face red as the apple sitting on Miss
Nelson's desk.

"What is it, William?" our teacher asked, turning
from her ciphering on the blackboard.

"Mr. Stofer's sent me to tell you—Virginia's
seceded from the Union!" William grinned like it
was real good news, but Miss Nelson's face went to
the color of her chalk.

"Seceded? Are you sure?" asked Miss Nelson.

Whispers and mumbles came from all around the room. My sister Emma, who looked just like Mama anyway, 'specially since she turned fifteen, wore the exact same expression Mama does when she hears any sort of bad news: her mouth in a little "o" and her brows scrunched close together. My brothers Will and Tommy, sitting side-by-side in the back of the room, could hardly stay in their seats. Their eyes sparkled with pleasure as they leaned their blond heads together. They was partial to any kind of excitement, good or bad.

"Yes, ma'am, I'm sure," William told her. "It's just come over the telegraph. The Culpeper Minutemen have orders to march immediately!"

I turned to Ferdy, sitting at the desk behind mine. "What's that mean, *seceded?*" I whispered. I thought I was good and quiet, but everybody looked my way.

Ferdy's eyes was wide and shiny. "It means we're at war, Lonzo," he said. "Virginia's at war with the Yankees!"

April 27, 1861

We'd been at war for ten whole days and I had not seen a single solitary Yankee, even though folks talked about 'em like they was everywhere. Well, they was not. And hooray for that!

There was other troubles, though, like findin' out who was stealin' chickens from Aunt Mariah's henhouse, and catchin' 'im. Aunt Mariah said me and Ferdy was just the men for the job.

A surprise spring thunderstorm blew through Culpeper on our way down to Winfrey, drenching us but leaving the air fresh and clean-smellin'. Puddles, yellow-rimmed with pine pollen, filled wagon ruts and holes in the road, givin' 'em the look of sunny flowers on a path.

But the rain made mine and Ferdy's job of settin' out traps harder. There wasn't a decent paw print

nowheres to tell us what sort of animal we was looking for, or even which direction the thief was comin'
from. It was nothin' but mud all around the henhouse.

We puzzled out the two likeliest routes a hungry
critter might take to get to the henhouse: along the
creek path off the side yard, on account of any animal's got to drink, or through the tight little fist of
woods that jutted into the backyard. That way
allowed for good cover.

The clouds had floated off to the east and the sun
was bright again. Ferdy headed toward the creek
path with one trap while I took the other trap and
studied the soft mossy ground at the edge of the
woods. Just inside the tree line, a row of gooseberry
bushes and other sorts of underbrush grew tall as a
man, and thick. The trap's chain swung loose in my
hand as I stepped over rotted logs and rocks and
through carpets of new grassy shoots.

A sour feeling came to my stomach so I tried
humming "Oh! Susanna" under my breath to ease it
up; but the song came out mournful as a funeral
dirge. I kept thinkin' about the awful thing that
would happen if I did my chore just right. Did soldiers feel that way goin' into battle? I wondered.

Before I'd gotten a stone's throw from where I'd
come into the woods, a tunnel in the gooseberries
caught my eye. It was just the right size for a little red
fox to wiggle through. I swallowed hard and com-

menced to setting the trap. *It ain't my decision to make, what's to live and what's to die.*

When the jaws sat open and was angled just the right way, I covered the trap with some damp leaves to hide it. Then I added a bit more leaves. And then a bit more. A trap was meant to be hid some, so the leaves was allowed. But I reckon not as much as I piled on.

I stepped away and stared at the spot where I'd hid the trap. It'd sure ease my mind to know I had no hand in maiming some little critter. I searched about on the ground until I found a stick 'bout the same thickness as a fox's leg. I tapped it easylike on the trigger spot of the trap.

Thwack!

The noise made me jump. The trap had sprung at the stick so fast and fierce all the leaves was thrown off sideways, leaving the metal teeth to bite deep into the wood. Splinters splayed out from the sides like a worn-out shaving brush. The outside bark was plumb *gone.* I felt sick.

A little ways off toward the creek path I heard the damp, muffled rustle of underbrush.

"Ferdy, I can't do this!" I said, kicking at the trap. "I mean, just look at this here stick . . . " I turned toward the noise, fightin' back hot tears.

But it was not Ferdy.

It was a skinny black bear cub. A little clump of wet grass clung to his furry chin. He stopped at a rotting log, sniffed, and dragged his paw through a caved-in spot along its side. The cub's eyes was rimmed in the palest sort of peachy pink, like the sky at dawn.

"Well, hey there," I said.

Blinking, he lifted his soft brown eyes to me and let out a little *hello* squeal. He licked at his buggy claws, belched, and went at the hole in the log again.

There was a sudden ruckus off a ways, and a big shadow blocked out the sun slantin' in from the west. The breeze carried an awful stink, like something rotten was mixed in with something sour.

I turned. And comin' straight for me on all fours was a big ol' mama bear. She was tryin' to get to her cub, I reckon, but I was dead in her path!

I couldn't move. I screamed.

Soon as I hollered, the mama bear rose up on her hind legs and bared her teeth. She was at least as tall as me, maybe even as tall as Papa. Bein' on her hind legs slowed her down some, but not enough to suit me. She kept comin' while I kept standin' there like my feet was glued to the ground. *I'm goin' to die!*

And here came Ferdy. He ran toward us from behind the mama, his arms waving in the air, his face red and his mouth wide open. We was all lined up: the cub in back of me, then me, then the mama, then Ferdy. I couldn't make out what Ferdy was screaming, 'cause I was either still screaming my own self, or the blood pounding in my ears was drowning out every other sound. My body wasn't working proper, that was sure. I burned with fear while my muscles stayed froze in place.

When Ferdy was closer to the black bear than she was to me, she must've heard him 'cause she slowed and turned his way.

And now that the bear wasn't lookin' at me, I heard Ferdy, too. "Holler and wave your arms!" he screamed. "C'mon, Lonzo! Holler and wave your arms!"

Finally I caught on. "Aahhhhh!" I screamed.

"Keep doin' it! Keep doin' it!" he said. "Now move out from between her and the cub! Don't turn your back on 'er, and keep hollerin'! Go! Go! GO!"

Ferdy yelled this right at the mama bear like he was telling *her* what to do—how brave he was!—but I knew he was really screamin' at *me*.

"I'm goin', I'm goin'!" I hollered while I beat my way sideways through the underbrush. The mama bear growled ferocious, first at me and then at Ferdy, givin' each of us what-for in turn, her big ol' paws in a reachin'-out pose to show off her wicked, sharp claws. I remembered Papa saying one time that one swipe of a bear's claw could take off somebody's head. Brambles in the underbrush scraped at my arms and face while I fought to get clear of them. "Your baby's just fine, now—you go on and take him home!" I screamed.

When we was clear of the woods, me and Ferdy kept on running till we was up to the barn. We fell into the warm hay, breathing hard. I laid my face in it, trying to get my wind again and listenin' to Big Moe snort in his stall. Normal things had never sounded so good before.

I turned to Ferdy. "That ol' bear was set on killing me, Ferdy," I said. "You saved my life!"

Ferdy sat up and drew his legs to his chest, resting his muscle-y forearms on his knees, and his forehead on his hands. He shook his head. In a minute, I saw his shoulders commence to shake, and he swiped one hand across his down-turned face.

"Hey, don't cry now, Ferdy," I said. "You knew just what to do and we got away safe! Things turned out fine." I had never seen Ferdy break down—he was always the strong one—and it was scary.

He wiped at his eyes some more and went on shakin', and I could hear him sniffling his snotty nose. I patted him on the back.

It was then that he lifted his head, and I saw he wasn't crying at all, but laughin'!

"You should'a seen the look on your face when that bear stood up, Lonzo! It was something! Looked like you saw the ghost of the Headless Horseman!" Tears streamed from his red-rimmed eyes and made wet paths through the dust on his freckly cheeks. He chucked my arm.

I hung my head. "You ain't goin' to tell nobody,

are you, Ferdy?" I asked him, shameful.

"Aw, o'course not," he said, giving me a lopsided grin.

I smiled then, too, on account of it was all over, we was both fine, and Ferdy was not crying. Aunt Mariah had told me a long time ago how Ferdy'd saved me from drowning when I was just a young'un. Now I owed him my life twice.

May 1861

By the time the woods lit up with dogwood blossoms a few weeks later, Culpeper was spilling over with men wanting to fight Yankees. More turned up every day.

"Why they got to come here?" I complained to Ferdy, my words echoing off the rocky walls around us. We was toting flour and coffee out to Aunt Mariah at Winfrey, going by way of the Deep Cut so's not to have to elbow our way through the crush of men on the main road. The Deep Cut was a gash through the hills just south of town where the train tracks was laid, and the shortest way to the inn.

"A feller can't even run through town anymore without knocking somebody off his feet," I said. I knew 'cause I'd done that very thing that morning.

"You kiddin'?" Ferdy said. "Culpeper's perfect for

matchin' up supplies and fightin' men off the railroad—seein' as how we're halfway 'tween Richmond
and Washington. We can group 'em and train 'em
and send 'em on up to fight, all from one spot." Ferdy
threw back his shoulders and lifted his chin. "Yep.
Culpeper's got it all. Everything an army needs 'fore
we set out to fight the Yankees."

I got a chill, hearing the way he said, "'fore *we* set
out to fight the Yankees." It riled me, too, how his
feet came down hard on the railroad ties. Like he
was *marching*.

"You ain't goin' to fight the Yankees, are you,
Ferdy?" I said.

"Humph!" Ferdy snorted. "Ain't nothin' I'd like
better, Lonzo, but I ain't old enough."

We went the rest of the way quiet while I puzzled
over Ferdy wanting to fight. What was it about
Yankees all a sudden that made everybody hate 'em
so? Shoot, if I was to think back a year or there-
abouts in my head, I couldn't've said exactly what a
Yankee even *was*. But with every new day, the word
got meaner in folks' mouths and anything hooked up
to it took on its lowness, too.

Later that evening, I worried over this with my
cousin Tish on the back steps at Uncle Daniel's.
Tish is almost two years younger'n me, but she's
smart as anything and has a funny, crooked way of
looking at things that makes near everything she
says interesting.

Like when I told her my notion that *Yankee* was a mean word now. Well, she let her shoulders sag and blurted out, "Mama's dumplings!" Just like that. Like putting them two ideas together ought'a make sense.

Mama's dumplings?

"What about 'em?" I said, wrinkling my brow. We was sharing one of Aunt Angelina's dumplings right that very moment—the only one leftover from their dinner. It was feathery light and melted on my tongue like nothing else that had ever landed there. But I couldn't puzzle out any connection 'tween Aunt Angelina's dumplings and a Yankee, and I said so.

"Lonzo," Tish said, "if folks in Culpeper knew Mama learned that recipe from her Yankee kin in Pennsylvania, why, they might not ever eat another one, hard as it would be for 'em not to." Then she gasped, slapping her hand over her mouth, and crept to the back door, nervouslike. After peekin' into the shadowy kitchen, she slipped through the door and came out again, quick-as-a-wink. In her hand was the little brown Bible she carried to church every Sunday. She made me swear on it that I would not let that secret out.

"Oh, come on, Tish. It ain't that bad," I said.

"Swear it anyway," she said; so I did.

"Being outdone in the kitchen by a Yankee woman's recipe might near 'bout kill a Southern woman, Lonzo. Mama says it's always been so, but it's 'specially true now."

I nodded, my mouth full again.

"Mama said to me, 'Letitia Jane' (and Lonzo, you *know* how I hate that name), 'if I ever hear tell you opened your mouth about that, you'll be one very sorry young lady.'"

Tish's imitation of Aunt Angelina was so good I laughed and sprayed bits of dumpling onto the porch. I wet my finger to make the crumbs stick to it and picked up what I could.

"I'm serious," Tish said. "Seems I can't hardly say anything anymore." She shook her head and yellow hair swished like fresh corn silk over her freckled arms. "There's some things that just ain't right going on. Mama knows it, too. Shoot, I think it'd do folks good to hear of something enjoyable coming out of the North. Don't you?"

Something crackled at the side of the yard, and I didn't answer. Lottie, the housemaid's daughter, peeked out from behind the old live oak.

"Hey there, Lottie, come here," Tish said.

Lottie stepped out from behind the tree, her eyes roaming over her bare feet, then the yard, and the porch, and Tish—everyplace 'cept at me. Her raggedy dress hung lower on one side than the other, sort of off her shoulder on account of it's being a mite too big for her. Lottie was eleven like Tish, but a good bit shorter, and scrawny as anything. Aside from big ol' Weezie, our own housemaid, most of the slaves was skinny like that.

"C'mon, this is good," Tish said, holding out the last forkful of dumpling.

Lottie crept over to the steps where we sat, her eyes pointed at her little brown toes till she got there, then finally at the fork. Tish poked the fork to Lottie's mouth, and she took that bite of dumpling. Her brown eyes got rounder and then she shut them while her mouth twisted and rolled over that bit of food. I thought she might lick her lips clear off her face trying to get the last of its flavor on her tongue. Aunt Angelina's dumplings was that good.

Tish smiled at her real big. "Told you so," she said to Lottie.

Lottie first looked to the empty plate, then to Tish. "Thank you," she said, soft. Throwing me a sideways glance, she darted off around the house.

Tish and me sat quiet on the planks of the porch steps watching fireflies commence to blinking. Presently I could tell, mostly by how Tish's eyes wasn't following any particular firefly, that something was cooking in her head.

"Lonzo!" she said, real quicklike and stirred up, grabbing my arm. "You come over and take supper with us tomorrow at noon, y' hear?"

"Will there be dumplings?" I asked.

Tish laughed. "Probably not, but it'll be worth showing up for. You can count on that."

The next morning I found out Mama'd invited all my kin that lived at Winfrey—Aunt Mariah, Ferdy, Grandma and Grandpa, and Papa's brothers, Uncle Jack and Uncle Edmund, to eat supper at *our* house. I sure hated missin' that. But I was curious as a body could be 'bout what was to happen at Tish's, so I kept my word and went to her house instead.

I got to Tish's near to a half hour early. Aunt Angelina didn't look surprised to see me. She sent me along with Tish's older brother and sisters to wash my hands, while she cleaned up the babies with a damp cloth in the kitchen.

Tish rubbed her hands together in the basin on the side porch, wearing a sparkly look in her eyes like it was her birthday or Christmas morning. Then she disappeared to the back of the house.

Supper must be awful special today, I told myself, drying my damp hands down the front of my britches.

In the dining room, Uncle Daniel sat his big self down at the head of the table, patting and smoothing his beard. Then, scrunching his eyebrows together, he made a show of looking all around his plate and under the table. "Now where could my napkin have got to?" he asked.

I looked about for it myself, till Uncle Daniel leaned over and reached for the top of my head. "Why, here it is," he said, grinning. The napkin appeared in his big hand like magic. "Lonzo, this is a napkin, son, not a slouch hat!"

I laughed. Uncle Daniel could be either a jokester or a bear, and I was glad to see today he was a jokester. If only Papa would tease with me like that!

"Where's our Letitia?" Uncle Daniel asked as Nellie, the housemaid, carried in one big bowl after another.

"Oh, that girl," Aunt Angelina muttered. "Tish, you come eat now," she called out. Even speakin' up like that, Aunt Angelina's voice was sort of soft. I reckoned it was so as not to be rude at the table.

"I'm right here, Mama." Tish's voice came from the doorway behind me. I didn't turn around. "And I brought a guest for supper."

'Course I was not a *real* guest, I was family; but I looked up and smiled at everybody anyhow. They all stared past me toward the doorway. I thought Nellie was going to spill the big bowl of salad fixings all over the table, her hands shook so. Aunt Angelina's face went ghostly white, then red as a radish.

What was going on?

I turned to the doorway, and then I *saw*.

Tish had got Lottie all dressed up in one of Tish's own Sunday frocks and was pushing her by the shoulders into the dining room to eat with us regular folks!

Lottie would not look up. I could see she was scared as anything by the tears making shiny tracks down her cheeks and the way she pushed backward against Tish's hands.

Had Tish lost her senses? Negroes was always to eat in the kitchen or at their own house; anybody more than two years old was mindful of that. I winced, scared on account of knowing Uncle Daniel's temper, and held my breath.

"Letitia Jane!" hollered Aunt Angelina. Seemed she'd forgot all about not raising her voice at the table. Her wide eyes cut from Tish to Uncle Daniel and back to Tish again.

In the short spell that followed, the place turned into an awful mess of tears and hollering and wrenching of hands. My stomach squeezed up in a tight little ball and my head hurt. I clapped my hands over my ears, trying to wait out the noise, but soon I gave up and slipped out the back door like a shamed old dog and ran as fast as I could for home.

I didn't see Tish for the better part of three days. I was running on the road past Jameson's orchard and wishing it was fall instead of spring so I could stop and get me a good red apple. I caught sight of Tish's yellow hair through the leaves ahead, and a pair of bug-bit legs dangling underneath the branches. It wasn't the happy leg-swingin' like is customary for Tish, but slow and sorrylike and woe-is-me leg-swingin'.

"Did you get a lickin'?" I asked her, panting and squinting up into the tree.

Tish looked away from my face real fast and off to some other tree or the sky or something far away, and her cheeks bunched up around her nose. I fixed my eyes away, too, so I didn't have to see her tears.

"No," she said. "Worse."

"Worser than a lickin'?" I asked. Whatever it was, I wasn't sure I wanted to hear about it. "What's worser than a lickin'?"

Tish sniffed, and I looked up into the tree. "They whupped up on Lottie," she said, half choking. "That was my punishment—watching *Lottie's* whuppin'."

I lost my breath for a long minute, hardly believing Tish's words.

"I'd counted on *me* getting' a whuppin'," she went on. "I figured it'd be worth it just to make Papa think. Grown-ups don't think near as much as they let on. But I sure didn't count on 'em whuppin' *Lottie.*"

Early July 1861

Lottie's whuppin' hung on my mind for near 'bout a week, but new worries got heaped on top of that one like red eye gravy on a Sunday biscuit, smotherin' it.

More and more men crowded into town every day, volunteerin' to fight. And the more fellers there was crowding in, the more there was fallin' sick. Now Aunt Mariah wanted me to come with her to Camp Henry and help nurse 'em. Me! I took sick myself over injured *critters*.

"Can't Ferdy go instead?" I asked. "They're soldiers, and you know how much Ferdy—"

"Lonzo!" Aunt Mariah cut me off. "Ferdy's got enough to keep him busy right here." She nodded toward the wheat field and pasture across the road from Winfrey.

Aunt Mariah's inn sat about three miles south of town near the east corner of Grandpa Rosson's land. Grandma and Grandpa had moved in with Aunt Mariah from their old farmhouse the year before, when Grandma's legs had got so bad she couldn't scramble out of her chair no more to swat Grandpa when he got on her last nerve; and Grandpa had got too blind to see that swat comin' until it was too late.

With all the crops, the long stretches of fence always needin' mendin', the chores inside the inn, and seein' to Grandma and Grandpa, there was always enough to keep everybody busy. I worked more at Winfrey since school had got out than I did at Papa's store. Anyways, Papa'd started takin' Will with him 'stead of me. Will had a head for numbers, he said.

Well, I knew that.

"What do I have a head for?" I asked Papa.

"For hanging a hat on, mostly," he'd said.

His words made my stomach ache. I wanted to sass him, to say somethin' like, "Papa, I don't even own a hat." But I was not brave enough.

I harnessed Big Moe, Aunt Mariah's half-blind horse, to the buggy. Across the lane, Ferdy leaned on his shovel and watched me load up his mama's remedies. When I waved at him, he just stared.

"I think Ferdy's got a hankerin' to go," I said. It

was mighty clear in my own head, but Aunt Mariah
was acting unawares.

"Ferdy's fence-mending today, Lonzo," she said.
The silver compass she wore on a chain around her
neck flashed in the sun as she moved about. "Besides,
the last thing that boy needs is to be in the midst of
a bunch of soldiers itching to fight. It's bad enough
he's heard your uncles' talk of mustering in." Aunt
Mariah shook her head and clicked her tongue. "And
in Tennessee, of all places!" she said. "God knows I
love my little brothers, but sometimes I can't see that
either of them has a brain in his head."

It was plenty common, local men mustering in. If
Papa and Uncle Daniel hadn't been the oldest of the
Rosson brothers, they'd likely do it, too. But Mama
said if they kept folks in groceries and dry goods and
shoes through bad times, they'd be doing their part.

I lifted the last of Aunt Mariah's jars into the
back of the buggy and tucked a thick wool blanket
around and between 'em so they wouldn't slide
around and spill her decoctions. Then I gave Aunt
Mariah a hand climbing in.

"Give my regards to the soldiers!" Grandpa
hollered from his rocker.

"Larkin, those men don't know you from Adam,"
Grandma said, fanning herself.

"Well they should, Miss Polly. Fought alongside
their daddies against the Injuns years ago."

"You don't know that."

I sent the horse a little slap down the reins and we started off for Camp Henry, leaving Grandma and Grandpa behind to bicker on the porch and Ferdy to mend the fence. I looked over my shoulder, wishing it was Ferdy in my place and me in his. I saw him kick at a clod of dirt, and I could tell he wished it, too.

Aunt Mariah and me rode along with just the sound of Big Moe's clomping feet between us for a while. Then I felt her take hold of my arm. For a small hand, her grip was strong. "What are you so thoughtful about this morning, Lonzo?" she asked.

I s'pose I'd been quiet a good long time, not hummin' or whistlin', which was my habit. I looked at her sideways and saw two crinkle lines in her forehead, lines what I had never took notice of before.

"Aunt Mariah," I said, my voice dry and crackling with the dust and heat. "Them Yankees fixing to set fire to Culpeper?"

She gave my arm a good hard squeeze and a smile spread across her face, easing out the lines. "Now where'd you hear that?" she asked. "I don't think they'd do anything of the sort. Culpeper's too important. We're smack-dab in the middle of everything."

Ferdy had said near the same thing, but I couldn't see how it kept the Yankees from setting fire to Culpeper. Fact was, it seemed even likelier they would do it, seeing as how the town was right on their way to Richmond, which they was probably itching to burn, too.

"Lonzo," Aunt Mariah said, "it's true the Yanks are bossy folks, and they'd sure like to tell us how to behave. They'll probably even try to capture Culpeper. But don't you worry. The Yankees are not stupid enough to burn it down!" When she chuckled afterward, her laugh had an empty sound, like after a guest at Winfrey tells a joke that's not funny.

It was near on noon when we crested the hill over Camp Henry. I pulled up on the reins and stared. White tents, rows and rows of them, stuck up out of the ground from here to forever like some Goliath-sized crop of pointy-top mushrooms. Several was set apart from the others at the far end. People, tiny from where we sat, moved in and around them like ants.

"Lord!" Aunt Mariah said, sitting in the buggy still as pond water, her eyes fixed on that separate huddle of tents in the corner. She held her bottom lip 'tween her teeth. A minute or two went by with her froze like that, and I hoped she was thinking on turning us back toward Winfrey again.

Finally, she heaved out a big sigh. "Let's get started, Lonzo. We're going to have a long day of it." She pointed to the tents separate from the others, the ones she'd been staring at. "Up there, in the corner—that'll be the hospital."

"Yes, ma'am," I said, and I let her know by my voice what I thought of that day's chores.

"They're just sick, son," Aunt Mariah said, her voice sure. "They haven't even seen battle yet. There won't be any blood." She set her mouth firm. "Besides . . ."

I waited. "Yes, ma'am?"

She looked me in the eye. "Your papa says it's time you got stronger and stopped behaving like a child. Do you know what that means?"

"Yes, ma'am."

"Okay then." Aunt Mariah nodded at the far corner of the encampment. "Let's go help those poor souls down there."

I gave the reins a slap, relieved that the noise covered up my sniffling. I blinked back stinging tears. Papa thought I was weak and a baby, along with being slow. How would I ever make him proud?

We'd got halfway to the hospital tents when the stink hit us in the face. I didn't have to see where it came from to know what it was. Privy smell and sick-stomach smell, like every man in that place put in his share from one end of his body or t'other. It stung my eyes and near 'bout made me heave over the side of the buggy. But I held out, thinking, *don't be no baby.*

As we pulled up, Aunt Mariah stood, her eyes roaming over the camp. Folks scurried this way and that, out of one tent and into another. A whiskered man, tall and skinny as a scrub pine, caught sight of us and strode up quick. When Aunt Mariah explained we was there to help, he led us about, saying which tents contained the men with dysentery, and which ones had the men with camp fever, and then he pointed up the row a ways at the tents what held soldiers with measles and chicken pox.

Aunt Mariah set me to toting her jars of remedies to one spot and another, depending on what she'd wrote out on the canning labels. I tried to take notice of how things was done, and not so much the smells what tried to choke me, or the nasty stains on the linens. *Be strong!*

Soon I noticed Aunt Mariah never sent me to the far end. "What about them up yonder?" I asked, nodding in the direction of the chicken pox tents. "Don't they need the medicines, too?"

Aunt Mariah ladled hot water into a metal cup from a pot at the cookfire. "You stay clear of those," she said. "I'll do them myself."

"Why?" I asked.

It was something I couldn't do with any grown-up person besides Aunt Mariah—question something I was told to do. But Aunt Mariah knew I meant no disrespect, and I asked her 'bout things that puzzled me on a regular basis.

"You remember when Mary Catherine and Will and Tommy all had the chicken pox two years back?" she said, pouring some white oak mixture into the hot water.

"Yes, ma'am," I said. "They run some God-awful fevers, but then they was just speckled up a bit. It wasn't nothing."

"Well, it's different when you're older; it's more serious. I still can't believe you didn't catch it back then." She handed me the medicine she'd just mixed. "Now do as I say and stay at this end."

"Yes, ma'am."

I stayed where she told me, dosing one feller after another after another with decoctions for the diarrhea or the camp fever. There was not even one soldier with a normal color to his skin—they was all yellow, or the color of birch bark, or burnin'-up red. One feller, his face like ashes in a bucket, near 'bout knocked me over when he jumped up and ran out the back of the tent. He dropped his britches and sat, his bottom hangin' over the edge of the raw, new-cut boards that bridged the open-pit privy. The air, thick with flies, hummed.

I ran to and fro for hours and hours till finally Aunt Mariah made me stop, just as the daylight washed out of the sky.

"Time to go," she said. She glanced down the row of tents and shook her head.

"But there's still some we haven't got to," I said.

"We've used everything I brought, Lonzo, and it's getting dark. We'll come back in a few days."

I took one last glance at the camp. Things was already bad for these men, and they wasn't even fighting any battles yet. My uncles and Ferdy all wanted to be soldiers. Ferdy was too young, and I was gladder than I could say for that. But what would it be like for my uncles?

July 13, 1861

A few days after helpin' out at Camp Henry, I followed Ferdy through the streets in town, agog over the costumes some of them Confederate volunteers wore. Maybe the men thought lookin' official would get 'em into a training camp sooner, ahead of fellers in plain old farmin' clothes. I couldn't say.

"Looky there at that one," Ferdy said. "Now *there* is a uniform!"

"You mean the one in them great baggy knickers and the tassled hat?" I clamped my hand over my mouth, trying not to laugh.

Ferdy scowled. "Not *that* one, Lonzo! He's just silly. The other one there, with all the shiny buttons."

The feller Ferdy pointed to looked like one I'd seen in a book at school—one of General Washington's soldiers in the American Revolution.

And Ferdy was right; he looked fine and proper.

"Hey, Lonzo!" Ferdy said, pulling me toward Coleman Street. "Let's go watch the recruits doin' their drills! Some of the units're already practicing out in the valley west of town. They ain't all got guns yet, but some of 'em's practicing saber fighting with sticks. It's a sight."

I didn't fancy watching anybody fight, but I reckoned since it was not real fighting and they wasn't using real weapons, it would not be too awful. Ferdy yammered all along the way about the excitement of the fights, and how the Army of Virginia was going to be led by the best generals in the whole country— the whole country *before* it got split up in two.

When we got to the hill overlooking the valley, we had to push our way through a swarm of other folks who'd come to watch, too. Some of 'em brought picnic hampers and spread out blankets on the ground. Fellers Ferdy's age and a year or so older clapped him on the back as we wiggled into the front of the crowd.

When we turned our eyes to the field, I saw that Ferdy was exactly right about the saber fighting. The men, paired off two by two, was stabbin' at the air with sticks and jumping forward and back, and sometimes ducking their heads when their pretend enemies jabbed their sticks at 'em. It looked to me like they was all doing some silly ol' dance. I didn't say that to Ferdy, o'course. Ferdy said how it was grand, and how he wished with all his heart and soul that Aunt Mariah'd sign the papers and let him go.

Just then, one of the men stabbed at his fighting partner and the man fell to the ground, hugging his stomach and hollering. When they carried him away, I saw blood on his shirt. All I could think was, *and that was only a stick!*

July 21, 1861

I was cold and shivery to my core, and when I coughed, my throat—no, my whole head—pained me. The light on my face gave me to think I lay in some bright and sunny spot, so why was I so cold? I rolled over to my side and tried to stand, but my legs wasn't up to the job. I kneeled and put my head to the sun-warmed grass.

Cannons sounded. *Maybe I've been shot. Shot in the head. That's why it hurts so bad. I'm goin' to die!*

I listened for the voices and heard them again. Closer now.

Yankees! The Yankees are comin' to finish me off!

"Ferdy!" I called out. "Ferdy, it's the Yanks!"

Then hands grabbed me from every side, and I punched at them and hollered, but inside my head,

I couldn't hear nothing at all anymore. Not even my own words.

Whole big chunks of quiet darkness took turns in my head with mixed-up sounds and fog. I heard Mama singing a lullaby, soft and sweet as could be, and then Tish's laughter. *I must'a got to heaven,* I thought, and I was happy not to be in that other place. I squinted to see the angels, or mayhaps get a peek at God. But there wasn't a thing in front of my eyes but a cloud, and when I tried to wave it away, warm hands wrapped me firm under a cover, all gentlelike, but strong.

Time floated by, changing the light on my eyelids. A cool cloth touched my head and a warm hand lifted up my neck. Aunt Mariah's soft voice said, "Drink, Lonzo."

Somebody else said, "Worst case of chicken pox I ever saw."

Who had chicken pox? I had to stay away from them!

Then the soft darkness took me away again. Sounds floated by like they was pieces of time, real things I could touch, but spaced apart somehow with nothing at all. I heard Christmas songs, and Papa told me to fly like a bird and fetch a package for him at the depot. I told him I couldn't fly—I couldn't even run no more; I was dead and gone to heaven. But the voice changed over, Papa's fading away, then Ferdy's, right next to me, whispering.

"I'm leaving to join up," he said.

"No, Ferdy!" I said, reaching out my hand. "Stay here. Stay with me, *please*."

"I got to help in the fight, Lonzo," he said. "I just got to, is all. You'll be fine now; your fever's broke."

"No," I said again. "Stay, stay here with me . . ."

"Take care of my mama for me, you hear?" Ferdy whispered.

"Don't leave, Ferdy . . ." I said, and I reached out to hold him there. But instead of Ferdy, my hand found some small hard thing pressed into it. I was so tired then, so heavy. I let the world fade into a peaceable quiet and slept.

The next time I heard noises, they flew at me with such a sharpness I wanted to back away. A crow cawed loud and shrill. I heard a rusted-over wagon wheel screech and a dog bark. Familiar sounds, but every one with sharp edges I'd never taken notice of before. I covered my ears and tried to smooth 'em over, make 'em soft again.

It was then I noticed a breeze coming at me, one wave after another, giving a tingly feel to my skin. I felt the hair at my forehead lift and settle, lift and settle. I opened my eyes a crack, expecting to see that same misty fog rolling in big clouds in front of me.

Instead, Mary Catherine's freckled face hovered over my own, wild-eyed. She waved the fan faster now, the one Mama cooled herself with in church. "Mama!" she shrieked. "He's awake, Mama!"

Her voice cut straight through my head. I held the pillow tight over my ears with my fists. Mama and Aunt Mariah rushed into the room where I lay, their faces a big mix of worry and gladness. As Mama put a warm hand to my head, the lines eased out of her face. She sat herself down on a chair next to my bed, some tears leaking down her cheeks. But aside from being wet, her face was happy.

"You gave us quite a scare, young man," she said, her voice muffled through the pillow.

I loosed it from my ears. "I did?" I asked, taking notice of my own raggedy-edged voice, how it was splintered and thin.

"You sure did," Aunt Mariah said, coming up close behind Mama and patting her shoulder a time or two. She set her hands on her narrow hips like when she's about to tell some feller at the inn a funny story. "Why Lonzo," she said, "you talked to the angels and sang like it was Christmas, you did!"

I remembered bits of it then, the quiet time and the clouds. "Papa told me to fly!" I said. "Fly like a bird. But I said I couldn't on account of I was dead. And Tish was somewheres laughing, and Ferdy told me he was going to fight. I told him, 'no don't go.' And somebody sang 'Away in a Manger.' It ain't December, is it?" I knew, someplace in my head, all those things couldn't be true, but I felt like they had to be, they was so real.

Mama and Aunt Mariah laughed.

"No, it's not December," Aunt Mariah said, a sparkly look to her. She flashed her eyes around the room, at the two beds, the wardrobe against the wall, the flowery-cushioned chair somebody'd moved up from the parlor. "All that happened right here in this room? Christmas, and angels?"

"I s'pose not," I said, those needles in my voice pinching inside my head. "Where's Ferdy?"

"He went up to Mountain Run to fish for the day," Aunt Mariah said. "He's not been himself lately, so I thought he could do with some time alone. It wasn't much past dawn when he left. Packed him up some cold chicken and a biscuit or two for his supper. The boy was so distracted he nearly forgot his fishing pole."

Mary Catherine crawled up on the bed beside me and poked at my right arm. "You got spots," she said.

I looked down and saw she was right. Blotches what could've been mold if they was green ran all over my skin, but in a fiery shade of red like the poison ivy Tommy got every summer. They itched, too, now I'd seen them, and I went to scratch.

Mama grabbed my hand. "Don't do that, Lonzo," she said. "Scratching will leave scars." She patted my arm like you'd do a cat, feathery light. "I'll draw up a tub for an oatmeal bath. That'll ease the itching some."

"Can I pour in the oats?" Mary Catherine asked,

hopping off my bed, her voice still high and jagged in my ears.

"Of course you can, Mary Catherine," Mama told her. Then Mama leaned over, fixing to kiss me on the head, I reckoned, and I reached up to hug her. But she backed off and took my hand.

"What's this?" she asked.

I was surprised to see I held my hand in a fist. I opened my fingers, and a dark piece of wood dropped to the bed, a carved-smooth and oiled piece. Mama picked it up and turned it over and over. It shone with the late afternoon light from the window. It was more'n half the length of her hand, the perfect shape of a man standing stiff and straight, and toting a rifle across his tiny shoulder.

"Where'd you get this?" Mama asked, her voice wondrous. "It's beautiful, Lonzo. Did you carve it yourself?"

I had not carved it, but it was right then I knew who did. "It was Ferdy," I said, slowlike, remembering bit by bit Ferdy's visit when he'd said my fever broke. Then the smooth, hard feel of the little carving pressed into my hand. "He gave it to me this morning."

Mama and Aunt Mariah turned to each other. Their eyes widened like a deer's on hearing strange noises in the woods, and their faces went to white. "This morning?" they asked, together.

"Yes, ma'am," I said, not knowing which mama I ought to be looking at now, my own or Ferdy's. "Least I think it was this morning. It was just barely daylight."

"Oh, Lord," Aunt Mariah said. "Oh, Lord, he's gone, El, he's gone to fight, hasn't he?" She spilled a river of tears down her face and clutched Mama, who stood now, too, hugging her back. They was a tangle of color, Mama's black print and Aunt Mariah's dark blue sleeves all mixed up, their hands rubbing and patting one another till I couldn't hardly separate them in my head. Only Aunt Mariah's wail hanging in the air above them said which mama was which. "My baby's gone," she cried over and over.

A terrible ache filled my chest while I ran my fingers over the tiny soldier slow and careful, how Ferdy must've done carving out its shape. And I felt the hardness and the softness of it all at once.

July 29, 1861

Ferdy'd gone, all right. He didn't come home that night or the next day or the day after that. I set the carved soldier next to the water pitcher on the little table 'tween my bed and Will and Tommy's. His tiny feet were so perfect-flat that, if I let go slow and careful-like, he could stand on his own, just like Ferdy.

I left him where I could see him from the bed most of the time, but took to slipping him under my pillow whenever I heard Aunt Mariah coming to check on me. She showed up in town near 'bout every morning after she'd seen to her guests at Winfrey. One morning she saw the carving there on the table and went to pieces, and it tore me up inside.

The first day I was allowed out of bed, I eased on a shirt and some britches over the itchy brown scabs of my chicken pox and tucked the carving into my pocket. From the stairs, I watched Aunt Mariah point her buggy straight at the center of town instead of back toward Winfrey. "Where's Aunt Mariah going?" I asked Papa, as I sat down to breakfast.

He looked at his plate like the answer to my question was writ there, then at me. "She's helping with the wounded down at Mrs. Flint's," he said. His voice held an uncommon hush.

"Wounded?" I said, my throat squeezing up tight. "What wounded?"

"The wounded men from the battle at Manassas," Papa said. I had to strain to hear him. Sounded to me like he was telling himself the news again 'cause he didn't believe it the first time. "They're in houses all over town. Filled up all the churches, too, every pew."

"But yesterday Will said we *won* the battle, Papa. He told me all about it, how we sent the Yankees runnin' back home. How they was in such a rush, they left cannons and knapsacks lyin' in the field!"

I felt for the carving through my britches. *It don't mean Ferdy's wounded. He's somewheres else entirely. Ferdy's safe—safe as this carving in my pocket.*

"What Will told you is true," Papa said. "But hundreds of men were killed, Lonzo. And thousands were wounded." He nudged a piece of ham with his fork, but didn't stab it. "Thousands."

I thought of the hundreds of men who came to town to muster in, and how they stood about, leaning on every fence and doorway, sprawled on porches, napping in the haylofts. Could it be there was that many of 'em *dead* now? And more than that, shot up? I could scarcely breathe, taking it all in.

It was a hot, sunny day, the sort I generally took pleasure in. But the bees buzzing in the hollyhocks outside the window took on a strangeness I couldn't name, like they was in a different place from me and Papa.

Papa felt it, too, I could tell. The pupils of his eyes was just tiny dots in the middle of the blue, and he didn't rant about the Yankees or slap his newspaper about. I knew then the world I'd woke up to after that fever was not the same one I'd got sick in.

Papa frowned and smeared a dab of honey on his biscuit. He brought it to his mouth, stopped and looked it over, then added more honey. He gave it a pure soaking. I watched his frown fade away to nothing while he chewed, then flooded my own biscuit. I reckon there's times when a feller just can't get enough sweetness.

By the end of September, Camp Henry'd growed twice as big as the first time I saw it, adding two sizeable hospital tents plus a kitchen. All the wounded had been moved there from people's houses, easin' folks' nerves a bit. Aunt Mariah smiled, too, but under that smile, her worry was no more a secret than the weather.

I was mostly back to normal myself, just tiny white dots here and again where the chicken pox used to be. Papa sent me down to Winfrey at mid-morning with the newspaper he'd finished reading, plus a sack of salt from the store. Aunt Mariah set me right off to the garden with orders to pick tomatoes and squash for canning, all of them that was ripe and still fit to eat.

"I picked the last of the pole beans, too," I said when I came in, three heavy baskets in my arms.

Aunt Mariah turned from the stove, the long wooden spoon in her hand dripping red juice onto the floorboards, and her eyes dripping tears on her housedress. "Did I tell you to pick the pole beans, too?" she hollered. *"Is that what I told you to do?"*

"Well—no—no ma'am," I stammered. "You said the squash and the tomatoes, but—"

"Why won't anyone mind me?" she screamed, and threw the spoon across the kitchen.

I ducked quick, dropping the baskets, and the wooden spoon missed my ear by a gnat's hair. Yellow and red and green vegetables tumbled onto the floor, the tomatoes rolling a ways before coming to a stop. When I looked up again, I saw the drops of juice from Aunt Mariah's spoon running down her pretty cornflower wallpaper, making it to look like the cornflowers was bleeding.

Aunt Mariah stomped out of the kitchen and on up the stairs. A lump rose in my throat, big and hard, and my legs went wobbly. I wanted to follow her and see to an apology. But how could I apologize for helping more than I was told?

I gathered up all the vegetables and put them on the table. Most was not the worst for wear except for two tomatoes, which I pitched onto the scrap heap from the kitchen stoop. I wiped the juice off the wall best I could. Turned out it was beet juice. I reckoned it would stain that wall forever.

Then I saw, on the table by the baskets, two things I'd missed before. Papa's newspaper lay open to a likeness of a Confederate soldier, a "Johnny Reb," as they was called. I'd seen this one around town some, comin' into Papa's store, and in church. He was a good bit older than Ferdy, but had a similar look about him, sure of his own mind, and brave. Underneath the likeness, it said, *"Joseph Embrey, first Culpeper casualty."*

Right next to the newspaper lay a red piece of paper, heart-shaped, with lace and a bit of ribbon woven through its faded-out edges. I picked it up and read, "To Mariah, My True Love Forever." Least I think that's what it said, as the ink was smeared a mite. It was signed, "Charles," with more smeariness, and a curlicue underneath.

"Charles is Joseph Embrey's papa." Aunt Mariah's voice behind me gave me a start. "He made me that Valentine when I was fourteen years old. We were childhood sweethearts, Charles and I."

I dropped the piece of paper to the table. "I'm sorry for pickin' the beans," I said. My voice came out high and strange, but I kept my eyes steady on hers so she'd know I spoke true. I was still confused 'bout why I should be sorry. I just wanted her to be happy again.

"Joseph came by the evening after your fever broke, Lonzo—the day that Ferdy left," she said. She dabbed at her eyes with a handkerchief. It had lace around the edges, just like the paper heart on the table. "Joseph told me he'd be mustering in the next day, and I did my best to talk him out of it. I reminded him what a good telegrapher he was, how he'd be so useful here in town at the newspaper, supporting the South, but safe, too. I talked and talked, but he wouldn't listen. And then . . ."

Aunt Mariah trailed off a bit, choking on the words still inside her. She wrung and twisted the lacy handkerchief while she stared out the window to somewheres far off, her eyes so full up with pain that my own head hurt.

"Then he said he'd try to find *Ferdy* for me." Tears dripped steady off her chin while her fingers worried at the lace. She picked and picked until it came apart into sorry little pink strings in her hands. "And I stopped trying to talk him out of going!" she said.

I looked away from her wet eyes and the ruined treasure she held, searching out some friendlier thing to rest my eyes on. But there in that kitchen, near about the happiest place I knew on Earth, all my eyes found was them sad, bleeding cornflowers.

November 1861

I raced through town toward Tish's house, breathing in the cold air through my neck scarf and then out into the wool. The fighting had moved north since the end of summer, and with hardly no soldiers about, I felt like a rabbit loosed from a cage. The carving Ferdy'd made slapped against my leg through the deep pocket of my trousers. I was getting faster day by day; I knew it.

Nearing Uncle Daniel's big house, I slowed to catch my breath and saw Lottie's daddy, Jacob, in the side yard. He leaned the handle of the wood-chopping mallet against one leg and rubbed his brown hands together fast. I could see his long-handle drawers through the torn knee of his britches. They had a hole in 'em, too.

Jacob saw me and grinned, showing his big horsey teeth. "Hey, Mista Lonza," he called.

I waved. "Hey, Jacob." Near 'bout every time I saw Jacob, I thought of a horse. But it was not so much on account of them teeth. Jacob had taught me to ride after Papa and Uncle Daniel had flat-out gave up.

I remembered it clear as anything. The uncommon hot spring day. How Papa lifted his hat and ran a hand over his head. How he muttered, his face confounded, 'fore he stomped off to the barn leaving me perched atop Jonah hollerin' "Giddyup!", my nerves all a-jangle. But Jonah would not budge.

Soon, Jacob came out and rubbed Jonah's neck and told me, "Lonza, hosses doesn't hear what you say wid yo' mouth. You got to talk to 'em wid all the rest of you. Stop tellin' him you a tangle o' balin' wire and tell him you a sack of taters."

It worked. 'Fore long, Jonah trotted around the yard a bit with me flopping up and down on his back. I got the feeling it was Jacob being there, all soft-voiced and soothing, what made it a mite easier for me to pretend I was that sack of taters.

Now Uncle Daniel stepped out onto the front porch. "Chop half a cord, Jacob, and don't dally about it," he said. Then, to me, "You here for Letitia, Lonzo?"

"Yessir," I said. "I came by to see if she wants to

go with me to Winfrey. Papa's sent me to help Aunt Mariah."

"Well, come on in and warm yourself," he said.

I watched Jacob fight a hunk of wood onto the chopping stump. "If it's all the same to you, sir, I'll wait out here with Jacob."

"Suit yourself," Uncle Daniel said, looking to the side yard. "Just don't slow him down." Then he went inside.

I watched Jacob tap an iron wedge into the short log he'd set up on the stump. He coughed, raspy, like he had the croup.

"You all right?" I asked, coming closer. Mary Catherine had got mighty sick last winter with the croup, and Jacob sounded that same way.

Jacob nodded. "'Tain't no worser than usual," he said. "No cause to fret."

When I got up close, though, I saw Jacob's skin was *not* his usual. It had a gray look, like ashes from the stove.

"You got another mallet?" I asked.

He nodded toward the shed.

I fetched the mallet, thinking on how I'd be getting faster *and* stronger today. I was muscling up like a workhorse, and Papa was sure to take notice soon as the weather warmed and my arms showed again. Jacob nodded, and I brought the mallet down hard from the other side of the stump. The sound was good and solid, and even though it was on the loud side of things, it had a measure of heat and strength I did not mind. Jacob followed with a stroke of his own, and then I swung again. The log split clean.

We fell into a good rhythm, Jacob and me. He took up humming a song under his breath while we worked, and when I remembered the words, I joined in:

> When the sun come back and the first quail call,
> Follow the drinkin' gourd;
> For the ol' man's waitin' for to carry you to freedom,
> If you follow the drinkin' gourd.

I had to chuckle after I sang them last words. They sure was silly; everybody knew a drinking gourd couldn't go no place less'n a body took it there himself, and so how could he follow it? Jacob must've thought they was awful funny, too, 'cause he took on a laughing fit. And that laughing fit turned into a coughing fit. Jacob got flat-out choked. I helped him get to the side-door stoop where, by and by, he settled his self down.

"You think that song's funny, too?" I asked, wrapping my scarf about his neck and ears.

"If'n you only knowed how funny it be, Lonza," he said. "A freckle-face white boy like you, sangin' dem words." He shook his head and chuckled some more, shrinking his fuzzy head down into my scarf like a turtle hiding from a hound dog.

"You need to rest, Jacob," I said.

"Ain't no rest fo' a nigger, Mista Lonza," he said. "You know dat. Mah rest'll come when I see th' Lord."

I finished off the last logs, wondering to myself if the darkies had a different heaven, a place away from white folks. That'd make sense, I reckoned. It might be the only way God could see they got any rest a'tall.

While I stacked up the pieces of firewood, the back door banged open and Tish came out. She hugged her coat around her and pushed her scarf up over her mouth. "Jacob, Nellie said to send you in for supper," she hollered through the scarf.

Jacob started off, then stopped short. He pulled my scarf off, looked on it kindly, and held it out. "Near 'bout forgot," he said.

I looked at Tish all bundled up, then at Jacob with his holes. I remembered Lottie's whuppin' for coming to the white folks table. I didn't want Jacob to get a whuppin', too, and I knew he would if he took to wearin' a white boy's clothes.

I went to Jacob and reached for the scarf. Then, making sure we wasn't seen from any window, I straightened it out a mite, wound it around his neck again, pulling up the collar of his tattered coat to cover it up. I tucked in the ends, so a body could not see it even if he was standing right there next to Jacob. The hairs on my neck stood up. "You keep it hid, y'hear?" I said.

We stood there staring back and forth a bit. Then Tish spoke up.

"Go on now and get your supper," she said.

Jacob nodded. "Yes'm," he said. While he hurried to the house, he sang low, "When the sun come back and the first quail call . . ."

I grinned and joined in again, "Follow the drinkin' gourd . . ."

Tish stared at me a spell before she started for the road. I followed, a snowflake or two swirling in circles 'round about us. We walked at a good clip toward Winfrey, listening to the skittering noises of squirrels and rabbits in the woods and our steps on the dry grass. Tish was quiet as them snowflakes.

Is she mad 'cause I gave Jacob my scarf? He'll keep it hid, I know he will. He won't get a whuppin' like Lottie did.

"Tish—" I started to explain, but she butted in.

"You know that song's 'bout escaping, don't you?"

Her thought surprised me. "'The Drinkin' Gourd'?" I asked. I shook my head. Why'd everybody all a sudden think a vegetable could walk about on its own? It didn't make no sense. "What's it s'posed to be escaping from?" I asked.

"It ain't about a drinking gourd escaping," Tish said. "It's about slaves escaping. I heard Mama talking to . . ." Tish trailed off like she forgot her next words.

I waited for her to remember who Aunt

Angelina'd been talking to 'bout slaves escaping, but we was clear past Jameson's orchard when she spoke again. "You know 'bout Uncle Edmund and Uncle Jack?"

"Know what about 'em?" I asked.

"They mustered in," she said. "Left last night for Tennessee."

January 1862

From my bed, I listened to Papa and Mama talk in their room. "Elvira, stop your worrying," Papa said, "Mariah may be a small woman, but she's strong. And she's been through hard times before."

"*Hard times*, Bernard? Just a few months ago, she had three strong men to help run a busy inn and a farm, and to care for your parents. Grandma and Grandpa are getting feebler by the day, you know. Now there's no one to help Mariah with any of it. These are a little more than *hard times*!" Mama talked in a voice softer than Papa's, but stubborn.

"She'll manage, I tell you. Look how she raised Ferdy all alone when John died. Besides, with the store to run, I don't have the time to run out to Winfrey all the time."

"You could give her a day's labor now and then,"

Mama said. "Let Lonzo and Will take some days at the store."

Aunt Mariah's steps was already measured and sad since Ferdy'd gone. What if she stopped moving for good?

I lay there listening and staring out at the winter sky through a gap in the window curtains. The snow had moved through, and the half-moon hung in the blackness like one side of Papa's reading spectacles. Even with a lens that big, though, there was some things I reckoned he'd never see.

"Humph!" Papa said. "Will might be useful, but you know how Lonzo is with tallying a few figures. By the time he added up a customer's bill, the prices would've gone up twice!"

"Lonzo does the best he can!" Mama said. "Good gracious, Bernard! Why must you expect so very much of everyone?"

Mama's question hung in the air, the quiet stretching out all around it, soft, but cold as the blanket of fresh snow outside. I turned on my back, pulled the quilt up to my chin, and stared at the shadows of bare branches, their crooked lines shivering, on the walls.

Tears sprang to my eyes, and in the darkness, where nobody 'cept God could see me, I burned with shame.

Papa's sharp voice cut through the stillness again. "I only expect the best," he said. "That's all."

I turned back to the window and wiped hot tears away with my sleeve. *I'll get better at everything then; he'll see. I'll set my wits to work. I'll sweat out my best job for Papa at every turn, that's what I'll do. Soon enough, I'll make him proud.*

There was a rustling sound, and the light from Mama and Papa's room disappeared. I squinched my eyes and prayed. *I'll do anything you want, God, just please make me faster and stronger and smarter.*

Sometime in the night I dreamed I was a baby eagle thrown from the nest. I felt myself falling and falling, and I woke in the morning, shivering, on the floor.

Mid-February 1862

Mama partly got her way, 'cause even though Papa did not go out to Winfrey his own self to help with chores, he sent me the very next morning after Uncle Jack and Uncle Edmund left.

I went four or five days a week from then on, too. I'd get up and dressed, then dress Abner for Mama on account of he was a handful for everybody 'cept me. After that, I'd bring up wash water or do the chores what was too heavy for Mama and Weezie. Weezie'd hand me a ham biscuit or two, which I'd eat in two bites each while she scolded me for it. Then I'd run out to Winfrey and work till the late afternoon sun threw long shadows on the ground. Some days I felt like I knew the way so good I could run along the railroad ties through the Deep Cut with my eyes shut, hittin' just the ties and dodgin' the gravel patches in between.

Papa turned up right 'bout Aunt Mariah; she'd woke up stronger 'stead of weaker after Uncle Jack and Uncle Edmund left. She wasn't jolly, laughing and singing; but overnight, it was like she'd throwed a shoe at herself the same way she used to do at Ferdy when he sassed, saying to herself, *this ain't no way to carry on.* She hardly stopped moving, catching up with chores she'd put off since Ferdy'd been gone. When I struggled to keep up, she said to me, "Have some faith, Lonzo. The Lord helps them that help themselves."

Well, the Lord had some catching up to do with *her*, the way she worked. Here it was the middle of February and she was still a'going. I reckon she meant to make her body so tired of a day that she wouldn't have no time to think, when the sun went down, what might could happen to Ferdy or Uncle Jack or Uncle Edmund out there in the wildness of the world.

We'd just got the mornin' chores finished when Aunt Mariah had me harness up Big Moe for a ride into town for supplies. The reins firm in her hands, she lit out. And she lit out *fast*.

"Aunt Mariah," I shouted over the clomping of hooves, "Ain't you worried 'bout Big Moe? He's not used to running full-out." Running fast was one thing, but running fast and blind in one eye had to be a pure terror. I was sorry for that horse.

Aunt Mariah shook her head and kept pushing him hard toward town. I hung on tight so's not to get flung from the wagon, and gritted my teeth.

Big Moe, shaggy in his winter coat, snorted as Aunt Mariah reined him in by Papa's store. I jumped from the wagon and helped her down, happy to know the ride was over and she couldn't go near that fast on the way back on account of hauling a load of goods for the inn.

"'Morning, Mariah," Papa boomed, coming out from behind the counter. "How's everything at Winfrey?" He touched her shoulder, quick-and-it-was-done, leaving Aunt Mariah leaning into a hug that wasn't there.

"'Morning," she said, pulling back. She worked her gloves off her fingers and pushed them into her coat pocket. "Lonzo's got my list, but Elvira mentioned last Sunday that some new cloth has come in," she said.

"It has," Papa answered, leading her to the dry goods shelves at the back of the store. Seven bolts of calico was lined up side by side like a straightened-out rainbow.

I warmed my hands at the woodstove, then dug in my pocket for the list. *Salt, one pound* was the first thing written there.

The bell on the door jangled and Mr. Stofer hurried in, the worn leather mailbag over his shoulder. He nodded to Papa.

Papa raised a finger, then said to Aunt Mariah, "Let me know when you've decided which ones you want me to cut." Before he joined Mr. Stofer at the counter, Papa touched her shoulder again. This time Aunt Mariah did not lean in.

At the front of the store, Mr. Stofer whispered something in Papa's ear while I weighed out some salt on the scale, adding a little at a time, trying to get it to just a pound. When it got close, I watched the needle good, pouring slow. All a sudden, a big *whoop* came out of Papa, and I jumped, dumping salt all over the counter.

"Aw, shucks!" I said, then clamped my hand over my mouth.

But Papa didn't take notice. He opened the door for Mr. Stofer, a few pieces of mail in his hand, and then, smiling big, he hurried behind the counter.

I scooped the salt back into the bin and started to measure again.

Papa made a show of shuffling the mail Mr. Stofer'd just brought, plunking one piece after another on the countertop, muttering names and making piles, till he came to one particular piece. "Well, what have we here?" he said. He stretched out his arm, reading the name on a small envelope. "Mariah Rosson, Culpeper, Virginia."

Aunt Mariah froze right there at the dry goods

counter, her fingers resting on a bolt of green calico. She lifted her head.

"Why, I don't believe I know any such resident, do you, Lonzo?"

I looked at him. "Sure, Papa, it's . . ." But when I saw how Papa's eyes peeked over his spectacles right at Aunt Mariah while he said the words to me, I knew he was joking. I grinned. "I mean, no, sir," I said, "that name don't ring a bell a'tall!"

Aunt Mariah rushed to the counter and swiped the envelope from Papa's hand. Trembling a mite, she clutched it to her heart, then drew it away to see her name, then clutched it to her again. Her eyes was full up with tears.

"Well go ahead, open it!" Papa said. "If it came all the way from Tennessee, it must be important."

Aunt Mariah gave Papa and me a quick smile and tore open the envelope. Her eyes spilled slow tears as they raced back and forth across the page. She made little noises while she read: hums, and sighs, and once, a giggle.

"Well, how *are* our little brothers?" Papa asked, crossing his arms.

Aunt Mariah sniffled. "Jack and Edmund are still together!" she said. Without taking her eyes off that bit of paper, she rooted about in her drawstring purse till she pulled out a handkerchief. She dabbed at her wet cheeks. "Jack wrote the letter—you know Edmund, he'd mean to, but he'd never get around to it." She laughed a bit, the first real laugh I'd heard out of her in a good long time. She looked up, her eyes flashing happiness all over me and Papa.

"Aren't you going to read it to us?" Papa asked.

"Oh, of course!" Aunt Mariah cleared her throat and stood tall. "'Dear Mariah,'" she began. "'I hope this letter finds you well. Edmund and I are stationed at Fort Donelson, high on a bluff above the Cumberland River. I am a lookout, posted most times in a turret facing northeast. I have a beautiful view of the mountains and the river.

"'Edmund mans a cannon below. If a Union gunboat approaches, it is I who will spot it and sound the alarm, and Edmund who will sink it and save the fort. The Rosson brothers will save the day!

"'So far, it has been quiet. Sometimes, when I am sure there is no threat afloat, I gaze eastward across the river and mountaintops and imagine that I can see my Virginia, and all the faces of my dear family.

"'Keep a fire lit, Mariah, as we will not be long in coming home. Your loving brother, Jack.

"'P.S. I would be most delighted to have a new pair of gloves.'"

We laughed then, Papa and Aunt Mariah and me together.

"It's a good sign," Aunt Mariah said. "Everything's going to turn out fine."

But just a short spell later while the sound of her sparkly laugh still echoed in my ears, I watched her

worry her fingers over the compass she wore. I reckoned it pained her that Ferdy had not wrote a letter
which ended, "Your loving son, Ferdy." Maybe he
feared his mama'd find out where that letter got
posted from, march herself there, and haul him
home by his ear. And maybe he'd be right.

Late February 1862

Some days, the troops came out of nowheres in great dusty clouds. One minute I could look out Winfrey's upstairs window facing the crossroads and take in the peaceful winter countryside, spread out like one of Grandma's quilts. The squares was every shade of green and brown, or sometimes white with snow, and stitched together with fences or hedgerows or narrow lanes. Then all a sudden, I'd see nothing a'tall of fields or roads, just shivery men and horses taking up every inch of space, mixed-up ants on a cold picnic blanket. 'Course the men and horses didn't really close in that fast; it just appeared that way.

"The lane's empty," I called to Aunt Mariah.

"Come down, then, and keep Grandma and Grandpa company," she said. "I've got to hang the laundry."

Downstairs, Grandma put down her sewing things, rubbing her swelled-up knuckles. "Lonzo," she said, "how about you fetch one of Ferdy's books and read to us?"

I bit my lip. They was used to Ferdy's good, smooth reading.

"That's the best idea you've come up with this year, Miss Polly," Grandpa said, winking in my direction.

"Oh hush, old man," Grandma told him, folding up her sewing spectacles. "Pick out something you'll like, Lonzo."

"Yes, ma'am," I said.

'Fore school had stopped on account of the war, Miss Nelson had called me a good reader. I hoped what I picked out now was easy, on account of even when I could say the words just so, I got some of their meanings jumbled in my head on a regular basis.

I ran my finger over the spines of Ferdy's books, stopping at the skinniest one. It had a likable title: *The Sketch Book*. I reckoned that meant there was pictures.

I pulled it down and sat cross-legged on the floor, halfway 'twixt the fire and the window. Grandma snuggled her coverlet up under her big arms, baring her swelled-up ankles. "Good choice, Lonzo," she said. "Start where the marker is."

I opened the book to page thirty-seven. "Rip Van

Winkle," I said. At first I read slowlike, being out of practice, but after stumbling over some long words, I got to going pretty good. "'The children of the village, too, would shout for joy whenever he approached. He assisted at their sports, made their playthings, taught them to fly kites and shoot marbles, and told them long stories of ghosts, witches, and Indians.'"

Already I liked the story, and I wished my Papa was like Rip. It was a hard thing to see in my head, Papa playing games. I read along a little further, sometimes not knowing what words meant, but it seemed like just when I was having a bad time of it, Grandma'd burst in:

"Oh, Rip's a *lazy* cad, is he? Fishing instead of working? Oh, excuse me, Lonzo. You go on now."

I read a little further, how this feller, Rip, had a dog named Wolf. But Rip's wife, Dame Van Winkle, was nasty to Rip and the dog both, always hollerin' 'bout Rip's idleness and the ruin he was bringing on his family. So he took a notion to walk off into the woods whenever he could, just for the peace and quiet.

"Well he's not just lazy, he's henpecked, too!" Grandpa said, looking my way and snickering. Grandpa's eyes was mostly sky blue, but there was milky white clouds in both of 'em. "That'll get you in a mess for sure!"

Grandma threw him a mean look, but Grandpa

went on smiling and rocking in his chair. I read on about the stranger Rip met one day in those woods. "'He bore on his shoulders a stout keg, that seemed full of liquor, and made signs for Rip to approach and assist him with the load.'"

"Ha! Here comes trouble," Grandma said. "Liquor is Satan's own water!"

"Let the boy read, Polly!"

"Go on," Grandma said.

So I did. I read all about how Rip drank so many sips of liquor that he fell dead asleep in the woods.

"What'd I tell you?" Grandma said. "Trouble!"

It was true. When poor Rip Van Winkle woke up, it was morning, and he knew, knew, *knew* he was in big trouble with Dame Van Winkle. "'He looked around for his gun, but in place of the clean well-oiled fowling-piece, he found . . . the barrel encrusted with rust, the lock falling off, and the stock worm-eaten. . . . Wolf, too, had disappeared, but he might have strayed away after a squirrel or partridge.'"

I was thinking, "Uh-oh!" for poor ol' Rip, and 'specially worried about that dog. Rip went to the village and found his house all broke down and the town full of folks he didn't know. Finally, he met up with a lady who called her baby "Rip," and it turned out she was his own little girl, all growed up. The townsfolk worked out how twenty years had been one night to Rip, and he'd missed the entire

Revolutionary War. While he was napping, the other settlers had started a whole new country.

Rip was the luckiest man I ever heard of, sleepin' through a war.

But Grandpa was not of the same mind. "Ain't that a shame," he said. "Poor ol' Rip didn't even get to turn the ladies' heads in a uniform." He chuckled.

"Humph!" Grandma said. But she smiled into her hand, and it was clear she'd taken pleasure in my reading, and maybe in arguing with Grandpa, too.

Just then a wagon rumbled up out front and I shut the book. The doors at both ends of the inn, the one next to the parlor where we was, and the other in the kitchen at the back, opened at once. Papa hurried in through the front one, a freezing wind at his back that whipped through the house. When he got the front door shut, I saw the worry hung on his face.

"What is it, Papa?" I asked, my face tingling. I rubbed my thumb back and forth across the coarse spine of the book.

Papa stood quiet while Aunt Mariah, rosy-cheeked, hurried in from the back of the house and hung her coat on the rack. She shivered and went to the fire, holding her red, chapped hands to its heat. "It's a mean wind today, isn't it, Bernard? I'll bet you're as cold after your ride as I am from hanging out the linens!"

"What's wrong, Papa?" I asked again.

Aunt Mariah turned to Papa. "Bernard?"

Papa's eyes slid from Aunt Mariah to Grandma, then Grandpa, and back to Aunt Mariah again. It was like he could not decide who he ought to be talking to. It was not me.

"Fort Donelson's fallen," Papa said.

Aunt Mariah eased herself into a chair, the color draining from her face 'cept for two red dots high on her cheeks.

"Fallen? Fallen off o' what?" I asked, muddled. Then I remembered from Uncle Jack's letter how the fort sat up high on the riverbank, and I took in a sharp breath. "Did it fall into that river?"

Papa sighed heavy and turned his stare on me. "Fallen to the Yankees, Lonzo," he said. "Captured."

Grandma reached out and took Grandpa's hand, her eyes closin' like she was prayin'. Grandpa grunted and opened his mouth as if to say something, then shut it again.

The biting cold Papa'd brung in with him was still alive all around us. *Was Uncle Jack and Uncle Edmund dead?*

March 1862

Me and Papa stood in front of Mr. Stofer in the tiny office at the *Observer*. The telegraph machine sat on the desk between us, quiet. I glanced above it, out the window, where soldiers passed this way and that. Southern troops was everywheres.

"There're not listed in the casualties, Bernard. All I know is, the prisoners were marched northward." Mr. Stofer propped his elbows on the telegraph table, rubbing his hands all over his face like he was giving it a good morning scrub. "I've been at it for days, you know. I've tried every telegraph post between here and Fort Donelson. There's just no more information."

"Any word on how many prisoners were taken, or where they're being kept?" Papa looked tired as I'd ever seen him.

"None."

Papa heaved a big sigh and let it hang in the air, filling the room with what-ifs and I-hope-nots before he put a hand on Mr. Stofer's shoulder and patted it. "I appreciate everything you've done, Alfred," he said. Then Papa ran his fingers 'round and 'round the brim of his brown slouch hat, slow and quiet, put it on his head, and walked out into the chill morning.

I nodded to Mr. Stofer and followed Papa.

At Rosson's Dry Goods, Papa packed up supplies for Aunt Mariah while I fetched Tish from her house. It'd be a good change, Tish helping out today. I didn't get to see her as much as I liked, my days bein' taken up with so many chores, and when Aunt Mariah said yesterday to fetch her after me and Papa visited Mr. Stofer, I was cheered a mite.

Tish climbed into the wagon and we started off. When we got near to Winfrey, Aunt Mariah came onto the main road, her steps full of grit and her heavy shawl pulled 'round her like a woolen cocoon. I reckoned if we hadn't been comin' with news, she'd have stomped all way into town to find out what was keeping us.

Papa drew up on Jonah's reins. "No word," he said.

"Nothing?"

"Well, there are no Rossons on the casualty list, but beyond that—"

"So they're not dead!" Aunt Mariah said, her words catching in her throat. She loosened the shawl a bit. "They're not *dead*."

Papa gave her a hand into the buggy. Tish and me listened quiet as rabbits behind them whilst Papa drove up the lane to Winfrey and told Aunt Mariah what else he knew. How Nashville'd been evacuated and most of Kentucky was in Union hands, and ports all up 'n' down the Miss'ippi River was cut off from supplies. Then he said how something called a "blockade" was choking the South.

"I can't find soap or wool or even hairpins, for heaven's sake. And Mariah, the prices for the stock I do get—salt or sugar or lamp oil—you'll have to forgive me for the charges on your order."

Aunt Mariah nodded. "They're not dead," she said soft.

Papa looked sideways at her and pulled up on the reins.

Aunt Mariah nodded to the path at the side of the house. "Got some soldiers in my dining room," she said. "Best go in through the kitchen."

I was surprised not to find soldiers in her kitchen, too. The Virginia House Hotel had 'em sleeping in the hallways at night. We was lucky Winfrey was just getting the overflow.

I set the last crate on the table and Papa spoke up again. "I'll let you know if I get any other news, Mariah. Alfred thinks we can still send letters to

Edmund and Jack at the Fort Donelson address, and they'll be forwarded to whatever prison camp they might've gone to."

"Praise the Lord," Aunt Mariah said. Her words was stronger than they was in the buggy, and I was glad to see her chin rise a bit.

Papa looked at me and Tish. "You two do your share, and head on home in time for supper, understand?"

"Yes, sir," we said together.

When Papa was gone, I helped Aunt Mariah in the kitchen, puttin' her things from the store into tins and cupboards when I knew where they was s'posed to go, while she ran in and out of the dining room with empty platters and bowls.

I reached for the last parcel just as she came through with an armload of plates, but when I saw what it was, I yelped and yanked my hand back fast.

Aunt Mariah stopped. "Rat poison," she said, looking at the small paper sack on the table.

"People poison, too!" I shivered.

Aunt Mariah nodded. "I'll put that sack up," she said.

She'd taught me to say "people poison, too" when I was just knee-high, so I'd leave it be. I reckon she didn't know that awful picture had been *enough* to scare me, that skull with empty eyes and bones crossing in front.

The first time I saw two little rat bodies gone to

mush after taking in the poison, my stomach heaved, right there in the barn. Seemed to me a rat had as much right to live as any other critter and was just trying to make it through the day. But Aunt Mariah said it was either them or us having food to eat, and she did not want their rat droppings in her flour for biscuits. I loved them biscuits, and I came to see the sense in that.

Tish and me had a supper of ham and Sadie's fresh milk before Aunt Mariah put us to work changing linens upstairs. We was not in the front bedroom one whole minute when Tish shook her head at the shiny saber leaning against the doorjamb. It must've belonged to one of the soldiers downstairs. "Ain't that an ugly thing!" she said.

"It is," I told her so's not to rile her. But I knew the saber its own self was a thing of beauty, gleaming and not a scratch anywhere. It was the job it was meant for that Tish took to be ugly.

"I'll be glad when folks see how silly this ol' war is," she said. Then she shook out a fresh linen and made it float, perfect-straight, down to the mattress.

I wasn't clear on what she meant, but Tish generally did not stop with saying one thing. So I tucked my corner of the linen just so, the way Aunt Mariah taught me to do, and waited.

Tish glanced to the doorway while she tucked her own side. "Mama's been asking Papa to free up Nellie and Jacob," she said, her voice all whispery.

"Free 'em up?" I whispered back.

"Shhh!" Tish put her finger to her lips like I'd hollered my words. She tippy-toed to the door and looked up and down the hall. Then she took the woolen blanket from atop the side chair and commenced to spreading it over the bed.

"Jacob's been ailin' bad," she said, all hushed, "and Nellie wants to get him up to her sister's in New York. Nellie's sister Clara got freed last year!"

Tish's eyes was sparkling like little candle flames.

"Uncle Daniel goin' to do it?" I asked, so quiet I couldn't hardly hear my own words.

Tish threw me a wide-eyed look with her mouth pursed up tight and looked to the door again. I took that to mean I was still too loud.

Then she let out a little breath. "It don't look like he is," she whispered. "They fuss about it back and forth when they think we're sleepin'. Papa says, 'How we goin' to get by without the money Jacob's cobblin' brings? And who's goin' to bake bread and mend and wash clothes if Nellie's gone?'

"And then Mama says how we could make out just fine if we all pitch in and help, and you don't have seven kids for nuthin', and anyways, how it just ain't right keeping another human being against their will."

Tish plopped the feather pillow at the head of the bed and gave it a pat. "So Papa's dead against it." A little smile tickled Tish's lips. "But Lonzo, I think

Mama just might . . ." She stopped and looked at me.

"Might what?" I mouthed to her. Not one little sound came out when I did it.

Tish picked up the pillow and fluffed it again, thoughtful-like. "Mama might—" Tish stopped right there and tilted her head like a bird.

I heard it then, too. Footsteps.

Aunt Mariah burst into the room, her arms full up with firewood. "You've not finished but *one bed?*" I jumped to help her unload the wood onto the hearth.

I did not learn what it was that Aunt Angelina might do. Brave as Tish was, if she was scared to say it, I knew it held a powerful danger. I tried not to think of it again.

July 11–12, 1862

"Wake up, Lonzo!"

A hand clamped my bare shoulder, the voice serious but low. "Pull on your britches and get yourself downstairs. Hurry, and be quiet about it!"

I froze for a moment, then sat up, startled and blinking. In the dim moonlight pressing through the dark curtain, the room was shades of gray and black. I could make out only shadowy shapes, skeletons of the notched bedposts and the hunched back of the chair. I put a hand to my chest to calm the pounding.

"Hurry, I said!" Papa's voice made me jump. "And mind you don't wake your brothers." His shadowy shape disappeared from the doorway.

I wanted to go back to my dream, where a raccoon had just climbed through my window and brought sweets to share with me. But Papa'd said come. I pulled on my shirt, britches, and boots, hurried downstairs.

In the kitchen, Mama stood rocking little Ellen, who'd just turned one. Both of 'em looked half-asleep. Mama handed me a lamp, unlit, and a small wooden box of matches. "Papa's waiting in the buggy!" she whispered.

"Where we goin'?" I whispered back.

Mama gave me a quick, hard squeeze, and held onto my arm for a second or two before turning away. "Just go on," she said, "and do what you're told." I heard her sniffle and wondered if she was taking a summer cold.

Outside, I followed the sound of Papa's grunts to the back of the wagon, fuming in my head 'bout being woke from a good dream to "do what I was told," and not even knowing what that was. Papa tugged one last time at the twine holding a tarp over the back of the wagon. "Ought to hold now," he muttered. Then he climbed in, took up the reins, and motioned for me to get in.

"Where we going?" I asked, climbing up quiet-like. Papa's horse Jonah gave a snort and tossed his mane like he was saying, *Yes, I'm wonderin' that, too.*

"Winfrey," Papa said, clicking his tongue.

Jonah shook his mane again, and started out.

It was worrisome, being out in the darkness with no reason to make sense of, and no sign in the east or west to say how long it'd be till dawn, neither. We took a roundabout route out of town, then down private lanes what had no names I knew of, and across a field or two. When the wagon got stuck, I heaved and pushed at the back while Papa guided Jonah.

Now and again Papa stopped, stepped up onto his seat, and studied the ground ahead. His goodly size towered above me, strong, providin' me a measure of safety in the darkness. Once, though, his breath caught in his throat, and he sat himself down quick and pointed us in another direction.

"What'd you see, Papa?" I asked.

"Shh!" The whites of his eyes glowed under the full moon. "Yankee encampment."

There was talk of Yanks being in the area the past couple of weeks, but I had not seen any my own self except one day at the depot with Tish. It was one thing to see 'em as prisoners, but I reckon it'd be a whole 'nother thing to find 'em sneaking through the woods with rifles.

We bumped and jostled till I thought my teeth might shake right out of my head, but finally we came up on Winfrey from the south. Our last road was the one what ran crossways through the middle of Grandma and Grandpa Rosson's farm, and I was relieved to recognize it, even though some of the fields was not planted full as they usually was in July.

We stopped at the edge of the woods and Papa

threw down the reins. "Hand me the lamp, Lonzo," he said.

Papa lit the lamp, passed it east to west three times, then put it out.

We sat, still as dew on the grass. It was clear Papa meant not to explain, so I waited. I listened to Jonah's breath and the crickets singing in the quiet, and watched while a kite made out of stars disappeared, bit by bit, behind the tree line.

Papa's stirrin' in the seat woke me some time later. He touched my arm and pointed down the lane. Just over the tops of the corn stalks, chest high, I caught sight of Aunt Mariah hurrying along in the moonlight and tugging Big Moe by a rope. Not long after, I heard the low creak of the flatbed wagon Big Moe pulled behind him, almost loud enough to cover up the cricket sounds, but not quite. When they got even with us, I saw digging tools piled up on the wagon.

"Let's get to work," Papa said. He got down and handed me a shovel. "We're going to bury some food, Lonzo. Now, look for areas under the hickory or white oaks, and stay clear of the maples and ash. Too hard digging through their shallow roots."

I'd never heard tell of burying food in the ground before and I couldn't puzzle out why a body might do something so foolish. But goin' up against Papa was not allowed.

I found a spot 'twixt two hickory trees and dug,

Papa and Aunt Mariah nearby, digging, too. We buried five barrels—flour and cornmeal, coffee, sugar and salt.

"Won't mice and squirrels and whatnot get in it?" I asked. We was practically planting the food in their house, I reckoned.

"I sealed them up tight," Papa said. "And even if they did get in it, Lonzo, it'd be better to feed some critters than some damned Yankees!"

When we'd stomped down the dirt good and even, Papa showed me how to cover those places with leaves. Time we'd finished, we got it so the woods all looked the same.

Pink was coloring the sky to the east when Papa went to the rear of the wagon and came back with a satchel. He held it out to me. "Your mother's packed up some clothes for you, Lonzo. You're to live at Winfrey for a while."

I stared at Papa in the early light, not moving, trying hard to read his face. I was not sad to stay with Aunt Mariah; I felt good and loved at Winfrey, like it was my second home. I even had my special hidin' place for my treasures in the black walnut tree out back. But what wrong thing did I do? Why was Papa givin' me away?

"Papa—" I started to say, trembling.

But Papa pushed the satchel into my arms. "Just do as you're told," he said. I thought I heard his voice catch in his throat, but I reckon it was my ears wishing to hear that sadness 'stead of any real sound. He got in the wagon and set out, back the way we'd come earlier.

Aunt Mariah reached an arm around me and leaned her head against my shoulder for just a second. "He just wants you here to protect me, Lonzo. I don't know why he can't say that himself. Now let's get up to the inn and start the morning chores," she said. Her tone was kind and knowing, like it wasn't no big thing to get given away. But I knew someplace down in the center of me it *was*.

After I'd milked Sadie, watered Big Moe, and helped Aunt Mariah collect eggs in the henhouse, I sat down to breakfast. But me and Aunt Mariah'd not got but one biscuit down, our eggs still in the pan, when a ruckus broke loose out front. Aunt Mariah ran to the door and let out a great wail. Shoving my second biscuit into my pocket, I ran after her.

The wheat field across the road from Winfrey— the one roadside from where Sadie was grazed—was afire! Out on the lane, Union soldiers, whoopin' and hollerin', made their mounts prance around.

Aunt Mariah took off across the lawn, headin' right into the burning field, screamin', "Sadie! Sadie! Oh, don't burn up my milk-cow! Sadie!"

Aunt Mariah's going to catch fire, just like that field!

I tore across the lawn and the road and into the fiery field, my feet burning through the soles of my

boots while I dodged the hottest spots. Aunt
Mariah'd headed for the corner of the lower pasture
that Sadie liked best. I tried to cut her off, but I
could not believe the speed on that little tiny
woman. I'd nearly caught her at the back of the
wheat field, terror rippin' through me at the sight of
the flames climbing up her apron strings, when she
stopped short. I slammed right into her, bringin' her
down to the ground hard. We rolled and rolled a
ways down the slope, past the fiery part, and came to
a stop, gaspin' and chokin'. The fire on her was out,
but bits of singed wheat clung to her ruined dress,
and her arms was reddened and her eyebrows burned
off.

"You're all right, Aunt Mariah," I told her, panting and shaking, patting her where the fire'd been so
it would not start up again.

"Sadie!" she cried into her hands.

"The fire didn't get down to Sadie's field," I said,
looking backward to make sure it wasn't coming
closer. I could see how it had worked its way toward
the inn and not away from it. Aunt Mariah kept crying, so to put her mind at rest, I squinted into the
sun, searching out Sadie's brown and white patches
in the soft green of the lower meadow. I aimed to
show Aunt Mariah how her milk-cow was just fine.

But Sadie was not just fine. My eyes found the
stain of her blood first, the size of it more than I could
bear, under her favorite stand of oaks and maples.

Her twisted body, no brown or white left to show, only red, lay in the middle of that stain, left to rot.

That was why Aunt Mariah'd stopped. I looked away and worked at holding down my turning stomach.

Next to me, Aunt Mariah took in some deep breaths and wiped her face on her apron. She'd just got control of herself again when suddenlike, she gasped and scrambled to her feet. "Mama and Papa!" she said. "And the inn! What if they set fire to the inn?"

I jumped up, too, and we climbed the slope, tugging at each other on the slippery mat of trampled wheat and burned earth.

When we got to the road, the soldiers had settled down some. They looked to be having a serious talk, gathered around their officers and making gestures toward the smokehouse and the barn.

Aunt Mariah pulled me into the inn, where Grandma and Grandpa stood trembling at the parlor's side window. "Stay right there!" she said to them, then staggered into the kitchen with me right behind her and grabbed hold of my shirtsleeve. "They're going to rob us!" she said, her eyes wild.

My hands shook, but Aunt Mariah was in such a tizzy, she didn't even take note of the stink them eggs was throwin' off, burned to cinders in the pan. I led her to a chair, then moved the pan off the cookstove.

"I heard it in town," she went on, pushing the

chair under the table 'stead of sitting down on it.
"They'll steal the meat right out of the smokehouse,
and make away with whatever else they can, too!"
Her tiny hands clenched to fists, then grabbed at her
hair, and her eyes narrowed.

She grabbed me by the arm again and pulled me
out the back door, her face red with more than just
the burn of the fire we'd been through. Around the
back of the vegetable garden, past the water pump
and into the smokehouse, she said, "Dump 'em! Just
dump 'em all!"

I watched her take a ham off its hook, carry it out
of the smokehouse and heave it over the fence with
a *splat!* into the mud at the side of the garden. She
gave a wild laugh, seeing the surprised look on the
soldiers' faces. I unhooked a side of bacon and
chucked it in the mud after her, and I laughed, too,
but inside my head I marveled. *Aunt Mariah was not
a woman to waste a thing if she could help it; but there
she was, throwing good meat in the mud! Was she losin'
her senses?*

The soldiers looked on, their eyes lighting up.
"They're carrying it right out here for us!" one said,
laughing.

He jumped off his horse and started toward the
meat, but the officer hollered out, "Halt, soldier!"

Aunt Mariah got another ham, and, with a
fierce power, thrust it over the fence. "You want our
meat?" she said, a crazy, thrilled look taking over

her face. Some of her hair pulled loose from its fastening and stood out from her head in all directions, fuzzy as a new chick. "Well, there it is," she hollered. "Take it!"

The soldier on foot waited.

"Mount, soldier," the officer said, looking sideways at Aunt Mariah.

"But—"

"I said, 'Mount!'" the officer hollered, turning his horse in a circle to face his men. "Can't you see she *wants* us to take them? They're poisoned!"

Aunt Mariah held her ground, still wearin' that crazy look.

The soldier followed his orders, but I could tell he was sorry to have to do it.

"Your ruse did not work, madam," the officer said, turning back to Aunt Mariah. "We are not so stupid as you might think!"

Well, Aunt Mariah took to laughing all wildlike again. The officer signaled and his men began to follow him at a trot toward town. I thought it was funny this time right along with Aunt Mariah. *Our meat wasn't poisoned!*

But we did not get to laugh for long. As the column of men took shape and moved away, streaks of fright and dread blew through me like an awful storm. There, in the middle of all them mounted soldiers, stood Papa's horse, Jonah, still hitched to Papa's wagon. Strange bundles lay in the wagon bed that earlier had held our stores of flour and corn-meal.

Where was Papa?

The soldier, the one who'd got off his horse for the meat, hung back. He smiled evil-like at us, prancing his horse in circles around Jonah. Then he rode, calm as you please, through Aunt Mariah's flock of geese, whacking the heads off as many as he could with his saber before following the others into town.

July 12, 1862

Aunt Mariah and me hauled the hams and the side of bacon out of the muck fast as we could. Through it all, tears stung my eyes. It was the hardest thing, not running hither and yon over Culpeper County trying to find Papa. But Aunt Mariah made me see why we couldn't.

"They're trying to starve us out, Lonzo, and I won't have it! If we leave the meat out here, it'll rot in the sun." She spat out the words like they was spoiled milk. "It'd be the same as if they'd taken it."

"But my Papa—"

"They're not after your Papa," Aunt Mariah said, moving fast. "They're after food and valuables. You saw the sacks in that wagon. They're looting. They killed Sadie because they don't want us having her milk, and she's too slow for them to take her with them. It's as simple as that. They could've killed us, but they didn't. Your Papa's fine."

Putting some muscle into it, she primed the pump. Over its whine, she said it again. "Your Papa's fine."

I held the pieces of meat under the cold gush of water while Aunt Mariah pumped. Then we rubbed more salt into 'em, wrapped 'em in a bedsheet, and hid 'em in the attic behind a trunk till we could smuggle 'em into town for my family.

I gathered up the dead geese that fouled the yard in front of Winfrey, sad tears drippin' from my chin, and hauled 'em to Mr. Curtis across the lane. Aunt Mariah said if they wasn't gutted straightaway, they'd go bad, and we did not have time to do it now.

All the while that I was doing as I was told, I felt a sick worry inside over Papa.

It didn't make sense to me, why I loved him so much; I just did, and there wasn't nothin' I could do to change it. It hurt to see his quick smile for Will and sometimes for Tommy or Mary Catherine, even when they wasn't tryin'. Why couldn't Papa do that with me?

Now I wondered if he was lying in the road some-wheres, bleeding into the powdery dirt. What if he called out, and nobody heard him but the birds and squirrels? *What if he's already dead, like Sadie and the geese?* Panic soured my gut.

I fetched Big Moe from the back pasture, thankful the Yankees hadn't got him, too, and hitched him to the hay wagon. All the way to the edge of town, I held tight to the weathered sideboards while Aunt Mariah pushed that poor workhorse into a hard and sweaty gallop. A splinter worked its way into my hand, and I watched, amazed, while a trickle of blood ran down the sideboard. I did not feel a thing.

We slowed and turned off the main road at the southern end of Jameson's orchard and found Samuel, Mr. Jameson's overseer.

"Cool him down for us, Samuel," Aunt Mariah told him. She handed over Big Moe's reins. "And hide him, best you can."

"Yes'm," Samuel said.

Then, after not findin' a soul at my house, Aunt Mariah and me ran up Coleman Street into town. Union soldiers stood on folks' porches and in storefronts, smokin' pipes and puffin' their chests out like they was all at-home and in-charge. I pushed my way into huddles of townsfolk, turning 'round and 'round to see all the faces, hoping one might be Papa, but not finding him.

Breathless, we came to Papa's store and saw the CLOSED sign in the window. Aunt Mariah yanked on the door anyway, but it was locked up tight. She leaned a shoulder against it, panting, then cried, "Daniel's house!" and pulled me into the street again.

Finally, I caught sight of the street where Uncle Daniel lived, its signpost showing through the leafy branches of the elms. Aunt Mariah squeezed my hand and I squeezed hers back. Slowing down a mite, we rounded the corner.

What I saw then sent such an awful deadness through me, I can't reason out how I covered that last stretch of road. Aunt Angelina and my mama and Nellie and Tish stood outside, wrapped in one another's arms and wailing. They saw us and rushed forward, crying out, "Oh, he's dead, he's dead, those Yankee devils!"

Aunt Mariah's hand slipped from mine and went to her mouth, smothering a low moan. I lost sight of her when the women's hugs swallowed her up.

I stood there feeling nothing but the emptiness of horrible change blowing through me. What would we do with Papa dead? The earth fell right out from under my feet and sat me down, hard.

Then Tish was there taking both my hands in hers, and I felt the wetness of her tears on them. "He almost did it," she said through choking sobs. "It was all set, I heard it myself. They were going tonight, and now he's dead!" She wrapped her arms around me.

"Tonight?" I said, pulling away so I could see her face. "We did it *last* night, Tish. We buried them barrels of food last night." I tried hard to puzzle out why she worried over food when the Yanks had killed

Papa. I couldn't make no sense of it. "Where is he?" I asked.

Tish stared at me, tears dripping off her chin. "Where is he? He's laying in the front room at Nellie's, o'course," she said. "Where else would he be?"

"Papa's laid out at Nellie's?" I asked.

Tish shook her head and looked at me peculiar. "No, Lonzo, *Jacob*'s laid out at Nellie's." She felt my head like Mama did when she thought I might be taking on a fever.

"Jacob?"

"Yes, *Jacob*! Didn't you hear? Miss Nelson's horses got spooked when some Yankee fired off his rifle, and they took off on a tear with her still in the carriage. She was screaming bloody murder, and Jacob rushed into the street to help. The horses swerved, but the carriage swung sideways and slammed right into Jacob." Tish sniffled and wiped her arm across her wet face. "He was a hero, plain and true, Lonzo. Jacob saved Miss Nelson's life!"

I sat a moment, numb, trying to take it all in. Jacob was dead, and probably Papa, too, and Yankees was to blame for it all.

None of the war's meanness had been a real thing in my life before that morning. I remembered them Yanks at Winfrey, laughing, and inside my head I saw Sadie's blood spreading out, and the burned field, and all them dead geese. Then, worse, Papa was gone from his wagon. And now Jacob, who would never hurt a flea on a hound dog, was dead on account of Yankees. Yankees who *said* they was fighting to free up the Negroes. A burn started up somewheres deep inside me.

"You all right, Lonzo?" Tish asked.

No, I was not all right. Nothin' was all right.

The women was gone from the street, so I rose up and headed for Tish's door. I meant to find Aunt Mariah and maybe Uncle Daniel, too, and finish what we'd set out to do, to find Papa.

I went inside. The parlor was dim after the bright day, and it took a short spell for things to take shape. I heard the women's whispers and sobs.

Then, there he was—Papa! He sat stiff and serious in Uncle Daniel's wing chair, alive as me. A bandage covered one whole side of his head, a spot of blood the size of a penny marking its center, and there was dirt and a smattering of blood up his white sleeve. *But he was alive!*

It was a peculiar thing seeing Papa in such a mess. He'd always dressed proper, and it was rare he didn't appear respectable. But bedraggled as he was right then, to my eyes he looked bigger than he'd ever looked before. I bawled with relief.

Papa looked away. "Get hold of yourself, Lonzo," he said.

Late July, 1862

There was hundreds of Yankees along that road to the Flatgrounds where Jacob was buried. Thousands.

From where they camped along both sides, I felt 'em watching us while we passed. The hairs at the back of my neck prickled. I was breathing raggedy, too, like I'd been running, only I hadn't.

Tish followed me, then Lottie.

I tried to stay to the middle of the powdery dirt. It seemed like every bit of space 'twixt me and them Yanks counted.

"Lonzo, calm yourself," Tish whispered. "We got nothing they want, y'hear?"

It was a long ways to the Flatgrounds on foot, but that was where all the Negroes was buried. I knew it was more'n two miles south of Winfrey, but I never had cause to go in there before. Cemeteries was things I generally kept clear of if I could.

Tish had been all set to take Lottie on her own, being brave to the skies. But Aunt Angelina had said no. "With Yankees all about, that's no place for two little girls to be walking by themselves," she'd said. "Lonzo, would you please go along?"

At first I'd complained, but then I saw Lottie's face, all pleading and sorrowful. What if it was Papa looking down from heaven, and not Jacob? Wouldn't I be brave enough then, to pass Yankees and see the place he was buried? I would, I knew it. I'd do it to make Papa proud.

While we hurried along, I cut my eyes to one side and then th' other, wonderin' what Yanks was like. From what I saw, they mostly played cards and smoked. A couple fellers sat writin', their backs to trees and a scrap of paper propped on their knees.

"What you reckon they're writin'?" I said to Tish, low.

"Just news to their folks back home, probably," Tish said. "They got families, too, you know."

"Humph," I said. "Well, *I* reckon they're saying how they was all brave and daring, taking hold of Culpeper from the courthouse down to the stables. You know they ain't writin' 'bout how they was brave against womenfolk and babies and old men! It's *lies* they're writin', Tish. All lies." My hands was tight in fists, thinking on it. "And it's a sure thing they ain't sayin' to their Yankee mamas, 'I myself was the cause of a nigger man dyin' three days ago.'"

By the time we got past all them soldiers, sweat had trickled down the sides of my face and the middle of my back. In another half-mile or so, I saw the clearing ahead and the pine trees growing up around it. When we was close enough to read the little wooden sign what said CEMETERY, I stopped.

Tish took up Lottie's little brown hand and patted it. "C'mon, Lottie, I'll go with you," she said, kind and soft. She pointed to a spot of loose dirt across the way. "I see the place, right over there."

Them two started out over the carpet of pine straw, sparse grass pushing through it here and again, their feet making no noise a'tall. A bit of breeze puffed around in the pines overhead, and a *chrip! chrip! chrip!* made me look up to see a papa cardinal wearing the friendliest sort of red. I thought how that place felt good, nothing like the cemetery in town, cold and gray and full of ghosts.

I followed Tish and Lottie then, still slow, but not so afraid. It seemed to me the spirits here'd be a friendlier sort, not mad at being dead, maybe even happy to get a rest.

Tish and Lottie stopped beside the fresh dirt and I heard Tish choke back a little sob. I came and stood behind them.

Lottie glanced this way and that, then darted off to the fence at the edge of the cemetery. She bent low to pick some black-eyed Susans.

"It don't even say his name," Tish whispered, pushing a small rock close to the mound with her toe.

It was true. There wasn't big white stones on any of the graves like there was in town, ones with fancy writing and carved edges, or low parts of ground for the mist to puddle in, early in the day. Only sad heaps of rocks gathered up here and again, and wooden crosses planted in the middles of some.

Tish crouched next to the pile on Jacob's grave and ran her fingers over the smaller stones. Picking up a pointy one, she sat on the grave and used that stone to scratch something on the biggest rock on the pile.

Lottie watched, one thin arm cradling the long flower stems against her, tenderlike.

Time stopped while Tish worked at the big stone, the pointy one leaving white marks just enough to read: J-A-C-O-B.

I saw, sudden-like, how fitting a thing it was, that name on the stone. It was Jacob in the Bible who used a rock for his pillow when he dreamed 'bout the ladder stretching from the ground up to heaven.

Tish blew on the stone, clearing away the dust, and straightened it till it sat just so on top of the mound.

Lottie laid the black-eyed Susans in front of the big stone, and stooped there a spell. I didn't hear no whimpering or even a sniffle. Finally, she stood and walked toward the road.

Tish looked all around the place. Slow and thoughtful-like, she dragged the back of one hand across her wet cheek. "This is where I'm gettin' buried," she said. "If I die before you, Lonzo, you make sure my family abides my wishes, hear? No matter what my papa says."

I nodded, my throat too tight to get any words past.

We started across the pine carpet and a breeze blew more needles down around us. As the cardinal called out again, I stopped to take one more look. It was a good place for anybody to take their rest, I decided. As I turned and walked toward the road again, the cardinal flew off, too, heading north.

August 7, 1862

Aunt Mariah and me was sharing a little bowl of butter beans for our supper when we heard pounding hoofbeats outside the inn. We stopped, forks halfway to our mouths. Then, like we was joined together at the ears, we scooted off to the kitchen carrying that dish between us, stuffing the rest of them beans in our mouths, chewing and pushing more in at the same time.

Yanks had cleaned out pantries and storehouses around Culpeper far and wide, some loading up foodstuffs on hay wagons and others filling up saddlebags with anything farm folks had left for themselves. Every bean, tomato, squash and cucumber, ripe or not, was gone—stripped off the vines, or trampled. We had the barrels we'd buried and some little whatnots hid in the cellar from last year's canning, but there wasn't much more. Aunt Mariah'd given the hams and the bacon to Papa and Uncle Daniel. "Take care of the children," she said. "We'll get by."

Kitchens in town was not robbed the same way, but Yankees banged on doors morning, noon, and night, demanding a share of what was on hand. It wasn't much. Supplies there was low anyhow on account of blocked roads and harbors.

Aunt Mariah hid our bowl under the clean ones on the shelf. We wiped our mouths, me with the back of my hand, Aunt Mariah with the corner of her apron, both of us still swallowing the last little bit when the front door of Winfrey slapped open.

Cavalrymen, five of 'em, lined up along the bar in the tavern room, red-faced and damp with sweat. The first three wore fancy decorations on their Yankee uniforms. Another feller, hairy as a bear, toted a fiddle case under one arm. Their stink found Aunt Mariah and me where we stood, back a ways from the doorway inside the kitchen.

Aunt Mariah tucked her chin in a bit and whispered to me sideways. "Best give them what they want," she said. "And don't rile them."

It was the same as she'd told me over and over the past weeks. Since the day the Yanks slaughtered Sadie, Aunt Mariah's wildness had got starved out. She told me that making them Yankees mad had only got her geese killed.

"We'll need four rooms for the night," one of the men said.

"I don't have any food." Aunt Mariah lied.

"I didn't ask for food, now, did I?" The soldier's smile showed little yellow teeth what looked like shoe peg corn under his bushy, mud-colored mustache. "I believe I said, 'four rooms.'"

"I've only got three," Aunt Mariah said. "My folks sleep in that fourth one, and they're old. Even Lonzo and I bed down on the kitchen floor when we're full up." Aunt Mariah edged closer to me and touched my arm. Her fingers held an uncommon chill.

"Then I suppose those 'folks' of yours will have to sleep elsewhere," he said, adjusting his sidearm in its holster.

Aunt Mariah's mouth fell open, but closed again on seeing that pistol.

A stirring quiet came over the room. My heart pounded. Horses snorted outside. Flies buzzed around the tables. Nobody moved.

Finally, an officer sidled up to the bar, the floorboards creaking under his weight. "You got whiskey?"

"Yes, sir," Aunt Mariah said, and the spell was broke. She hurried to the cabinet to get the bottle, and nodded for me to get glasses. We had just got a supply of spirits before the embargo cut it off. I wondered what we'd do when the whiskey was gone.

I fetched four glasses, all I could carry, and went

back for another. More hoofbeats thundered up the lane outside.

Aunt Mariah moved quick then, asking, "Whiskey or ale?" of each one. But there was not a speck of friendliness or respect in her voice.

"I'll fetch the ale," I told her, quietlike, and she nodded. I had a look behind me 'fore I left, making sure Aunt Mariah was fine. All them fellers watched me go. Every one.

I flew through the kitchen, then down the dirt path to the icehouse in the cedars. Taking the key from under the stone, I rolled out a keg and counted what was left. Eight. That would not last long. I shut the heavy oak door again, hid the key, and stumbled up the path, panting, my arms closed around that small keg. I was like jagged glass, inside and out. *Please, God, don't let 'em hurt Aunt Mariah.*

I kicked Winfrey's back door open, sweat dripping into my eyes, stingin'. I carried the keg in, blinking fast and straining to see into the dimness. Soon my eyes adjusted, and everyone in the room came to life around me, Aunt Mariah wiping down the bar and the others standing about, only it was more of 'em now. The one what looked like a bear took the fiddle from its case.

Another, who I took to be the leader on account of his cocksure ways, lifted his glass. "To the preservation of the Union!" he hollered. His voice seemed a mite high for a man. There wasn't no call to holler, neither; it was like he was giving out permission for the rowdiness to begin.

There was cheering all around, and the fiddler started in. Some of the men clapped.

The one in charge was shorter than the rest and skinny, and his thin, pointy nose and little eyes made me think of a rat. His hair was reddish blond, though, and I had never seen a rat with that color of hair. He played with a pocketknife at the bar, telling all those nearby, plus the roof and the floor and the air in between, how some gen'ral gave him that special treasure. The more excited he got in the telling, the more screechy his voice got. It purely set my teeth on edge.

I watched while he flipped the blade in and out, in and out. It was as fine a knife as I'd ever seen, even finer than those in Papa's store. The etchings on the silver handle ran deep, catching the lamplight now and again, and sparkling like Aunt Angelina's chandelier. The end of the handle was shaped like a horse's head.

Aunt Mariah set her jaw firm and pulled her lips into a thin, tight line. Her hand shook a mite as she poured him another glass of whiskey.

"What's your name?" he asked Aunt Mariah, running a stubby finger down the dull side of the blade.

Aunt Mariah pulled her hand back quick after pushing his glass to him, saying nothing a'tall. The others laughed.

I stepped in closer.

"I'm not going to harm you, ma'am," he said, raising his glass to his mouth. His Adam's apple bobbed up and down when he swallowed. "Name's Custard. Much obliged," he said.

I had to hold in a laugh. Custard! That man had the very same name as dessert on Sunday!

But I wasn't feeling like a laugh for very long, 'cause another of them Yankees stepped around the counter and pulled at Aunt Mariah, saying, "Come dance with me, woman!"

Aunt Mariah pulled away, but the feller kept at it.

"Oh, come now, just one dance," he said, and got her by the hands. His boots dragged and scraped along the planks of the floor with his clumsy steps.

Aunt Mariah's chin trembled and she stumbled some. Our eyes met and her look sent a panic through my bones.

"I'll dance!" I said and jumped in, taking Aunt Mariah's place. I pulled the feller this way and that, steering him away from the bar and Aunt Mariah. His eyes got big with surprise, and everybody laughed except for me and Aunt Mariah. I didn't want to dance, but more than that, I didn't want that dirty Yankee touching my aunt.

While I spun the feller around, I found her face in the room. She wore a look I couldn't puzzle out, but it was not a scared look anymore.

The others, Custard and all of 'em, appeared to be having a high time, laughing and clapping in a circle around me and the feller, and tapping their toes.

One Yank drained his glass as we passed by, and 'stead of setting it down easy, he hurled it at the side wall. It hit exactly on the likeness of Jefferson Davis, President of the Confederacy, which Aunt Mariah'd clipped from the *Culpeper Observer* and put in a frame.

The men all cheered when the glass made its tinkling crash to the floor. Custard, 'stead of dressing down his feller for busting up the place, raised his glass again, saying, "Aha! The downfall of Jefferson Davis at last!"

I watched Aunt Mariah while I thought "Uh-oh" in my head. But she swept up the glass, calmlike, and that Yankee did not see her eyes, dangerous and sharp as those shards in the dustbin.

When the music stopped, some of the fellers slapped me on the back, laughing big and saying how I was a dandy.

I wasn't feeling dandy, that was sure. I was scared and nervy and feeling like a moth-eaten blanket in January, doing half the job I aimed to do. There was no fairness to it, a little tiny woman and a half-growed boy up against fighting men with pistols.

But Aunt Mariah was frightful mad. "Don't you ever do that again," she scolded through clenched teeth. We set dirty glasses on the pass-through to the kitchen, our backs to them rowdy men. "They're mean and ornery, and they're making you look the fool!"

I took the scolding, hurting with every one of them words. But I remembered her pinched face when that Yankee pulled at her, and I was not sorry for what I'd done.

At dusk I fetched an oil lamp and helped Grandpa get Grandma from their bedroom upstairs down to the cellar. Passing through the parlor, one of the men nodded to Grandma, touching the brim of his hat, and nudged others out of the way. I saw a softness come into his eyes and it gave me a start, seeing such a thing from a Yankee.

Grandma said, "You can feign respect all you like, young man. Your officer just ordered us to the hard basement floor while a couple of healthy men less than half my age will sleep in my soft bed!"

"Yes, ma'am," he said, his voice just a whisper, and he touched his hat again. The others stared at their shoes or looked away till we got by.

I set the lamp on the dusty canning shelves against the wall in the cellar. Shadowy circles showed where jars of butter beans and beets had sat through the winter and spring. We'd hid the last of 'em under the stairs in back of empty crates to see us through worser times. But it was hard to imagine worser times than now.

I made a pallet from quilts that Grandma'd sewn back when her fingers worked proper. In one of them quilts was pieces of old clothes from everybody in the family: a shirt what had been Ferdy's, bits of Emma's and Mama's old frocks, a piece I'd seen on Tish. Looking at the quilt, I felt connected to everybody else whose clothes made their way into it. It was a magical thing, how a quilt stitched a family together.

I fussed a bit with the make-do bed.

"It's just fine, Lonzo," Grandma said. "You go on now and make up a place for yourself."

"Yes, ma'am." I sighed and took up the lamp.

Grandma sneezed. I gave her my handkerchief, kissed her and Grandpa good night, and dragged myself up the cellar steps. For not eating more'n a few beans all day, I felt mighty heavy.

The drinking and music went on a while longer before Custard called an end to it. Some of the men grumbled a bit, but soon took to setting out their bedrolls in the parlor and the dining room, the last ones taking a spot in the hall.

Aunt Mariah sent me upstairs to see to the officers. It galled me to set the pitchers of water in those rooms, and to see Custard lay that fancy knife on the crocheted scarf atop Grandma's dressing table, exactly in the spot where her hairbrush ought to be. *Damn Yankee!*

When all the men was settled and the lamp snuffed out at the table where Aunt Mariah wrote

her letters to Uncle Jack and Uncle Edmund, I laid
awake on the kitchen floor. Aunt Mariah breathed
smooth and slow at my back while I listened to the
crickets and a hoot owl, and the horses' gentle nick-
ering at the rail. A near-full moon threw a window
of light on the floor.

Snores rose up, one by one, and floated about on
the sticky night air. It was then I heard Aunt Mariah
crying, ever-so-soft.

I turned to her and my chest squeezed up tight. I
hated the awful trembling of her shoulders, the
harsh, icy blue moonlight falling on her crumpled
wet face, the pain everywhere I looked.

I petted her arm, soothing her like I used to do
Abner when he had a nightmare. After a time, Aunt
Mariah cried herself out and slept.

Presently, I heard the *creak! creak!* of the floorboards in the front bedroom, then a scuffling,
scraping noise.

Custard?

I laid still as a corpse while his heavy boots
scraped down the staircase, through the hall and
kitchen, and past my head on the way to the privy.
The thought of him crawling back into Grandma's
and Grandpa's bed made me boil inside.

Suddenlike, with nary a thought of the danger, I
flew upstairs to that room and snatched up that special silver knife Custard was so fond of from
Grandma's dressing table. Fast as lightning, I dashed

back down the steps, hardly alighting on 'em a'tall, picked my way around sleeping, stinky Yanks, and took up my spot on the kitchen floor. I was just in time. Custard clomped up the stepping stones to the back door and opened it.

Inside my head, my wild little gasps sounded loud enough to rattle the walls. When Custard stopped next to me, I knew he'd heard 'em, too. I held my breath.

There was a muffled *thump-thump*; then Custard let out a loud belch. I heard a scratching noise and a grunt, and he went on up the stairs.

Clunk! One boot hit the floor, then *clunk!* the other. I waited, waited, waited, the blood still rushing in my ears while I watched the moonlight creep further up the wall behind Aunt Mariah.

When I couldn't bear the fiery feel of the knife in my hand any longer, I rose up and eased the back door open just wide enough so I could slip out. I crept to the side yard, careful not to worry the horses none, and climbed into the farthest of the three black walnut trees that separated the yard from the south pasture.

Among the heavy overhang of green pods, I felt the rough bark for that opening, high up, where I kept my Mexican penny and a real Indian arrowhead. I pushed that fancy knife into the long knothole until it was stuck there good.

"Damn Yankee!" I whispered, and pounded the knife with my fist.

I climbed down and, quiet as a rabbit, bounded across the yard. At the door I paused and turned, smiling, at the almost-whole man in the moon. Me and him shared a good secret.

August 8, 1862, Sunrise

"What the devil?!" I knew who the voice belonged to straightaway.

I jumped out of my pallet and looked at the ceiling, following the angry sound of Northern boots scraping and clomping to the front bedroom upstairs.

Aunt Mariah was gone and her pallet was already put up. I quick rolled up mine and stowed it under the cupboard.

"Where's my *knife?*" Custard hollered.

A low rumble of voices rose up through the inn, some coming from those front rooms upstairs and some from the parlor and the hallway. Floorboards creaked overhead. A jolt of fear shot through me, leaving my insides aquiver and my fingers without any feeling in 'em a'tall.

When I made off with Custard's knife, I felt good and fair. I took something he treasured, the same way he'd snatched up our beds and our peaceful lives. It felt right.

Now, I wasn't so sure. From the time I was knee-high, Mama and Papa'd said how stealing was sinful. It was right there in the Bible, *Thou shalt not steal.* But did stealing from a Yankee count? And what would Custard do if he found me out? My stomach flopped around inside my belly like a fresh-caught fish.

"I told you, I haven't seen it!" came a voice.

More stomping of boots. More creaking across the floorboards, coming to a stop over my head. I could near 'bout feel the press of them men weighing down on me from above.

"Well, I laid it down right here"—there was a rapping-on-wood sound—"last night when I retired. I *know* I did." Custard's voice was lower-pitched and less whiny than yesterday, more like a mean ol' growling dog than a weasel squeaking.

The whole of the inn was stirring then, men packing up their bedrolls and cutting their eyes one to the other like they was thinking, "Uh-oh," just like me.

"Lonzo!" Aunt Mariah called from the side yard, banging around some metal pails. The hollering upstairs got louder. The vexed Yanks in the hall looked like they was dreading the next little while as bad as me. I hustled outside.

Aunt Mariah threw me a sideways look as she lined up the pails next to the pump. I knew that face; it gen'rally meant she was wantin' to have a talk. *Did she know?*

The handle screeched while I primed the pump. I was grateful for the noise; there couldn't be talk with that racket. But in next to no time, the water gushed out and one after the other, we filled all the pails. Too soon, our noisy job was done and we could hear Custard's ranting again.

"What's that he's hollering about?" Aunt Mariah's head tilted and her eyes narrowed just a hair. Maybe the eye-squinchin' was from the bright morning sun just peekin' 'round the foot of Mount Pony, or maybe it was from whatever was goin' on in her head. It was hard to tell.

My stomach clenched up and my face got uncommon-hot. I looked back at the inn. A bit of lace curtain fluttered at the bedroom window as that Yankee—a man we didn't even know—gestured with his fist in Grandma's bedroom. I turned back to Aunt Mariah, took a good full breath, and stood tall. "The little one name of Custard has lost his show-off knife," I said.

Aunt Mariah's eyes, red-rimmed and tired-looking, held on to mine for a long minute. I looked, but couldn't find a hint of fire in 'em. I knew then, it didn't matter if she found me out or not. She would not hold me answerable to stealing from Yankees.

I went back to loadin' up the water pails and toted the wheelbarrow to the back door. Aunt Mariah followed behind me, quiet.

For an hour or more, every Yankee from the camp cook to Custard himself near 'bout turned the inn on its side. They went through bedrolls, searched every closet, every nook, every corner of Winfrey, and that little ratty man still did not have his knife.

"No one will eat, or sleep, or move *one inch down that lane* until whoever took my knife returns it!" he screamed.

We was walking the grass outside now, my heart thumping quicker as I pretended to hunt with the rest, and watching from the corner of my eye while Custard tromped around under the second of the three black walnut trees.

Finally somebody spoke up. "Sir, may I make a suggestion?" I saw it was the one from last night, the feller with them strange, kind-looking eyes.

"If it will help to locate my knife, you may," Custard said, kicking at a clump of tall grass under the tree.

The feller sighed loud and rested his hands on his hip bones. "You had a grand time last evening, didn't you, sir?" he said. "I mean with the music and the whiskey and all?"

He had a peculiar way of looking away when he talked, his eyes roaming the sky 'stead of Custard's face. I glanced up, wondering if a hawk was over-head.

"I had a fine evening, Dempsey," Custard said. "Now, what's this suggestion of yours, so we can get on with finding my knife?"

Dempsey coughed, looked at his boots, then off somewheres down the lane. "Well, sir," he said, "I've been thinking maybe you didn't put the knife on the dressing table at all, sir, but kept it in your pocket . . . what with the drink and all."

"Then it'd still be in my pocket, wouldn't it?" Custard hollered, and yanked his pockets inside out. He turned 'round and 'round for all the men to see, makin' a great show of it, and getting all red-faced.

"Sir?" Dempsey said.

Custard tucked his pockets back into his britches.

"Sir, what if, when you went to the privy . . ."

There was quiet for a short spell, then some of the men standing back a ways let out some low chuckles. Custard glared at 'em, and they stopped.

Nothing moved, then. Not a leaf on a tree nor a hair on a head. Custard gave a fierce look down the yard at the privy, his face deepening near to the color of a plum. He bent down and picked up a green walnut pod from the ground, and with barely a glance at his target, hurled it toward the lane. It hit—*thwack!*—square on the side of the Yankees' mess wagon what held all their food.

"Damn, damn, DAMN!" he yelled, kicking at the dirt again and again. All eyes was on him while he made his big ruckus under the tree next to where I'd hid that knife.

All eyes except for Dempsey's, anyways. I followed where he was looking.

I could not've moved right then if cows had commenced to falling from the sky. I shot a look back at Dempsey, and he raised an eyebrow at me. We both watched, quiet, as my brother Will, who must've been out exploring, crouched at the side of the mess wagon as if he was playing Indians with Tommy. But Tommy wasn't there. Will was hidin' from the Yanks! And while I watched, he grabbed up a big sack from off the wagon and hauled it without a sound to the thicket aside the front porch.

Custard stomped one last time and punched at the air. "Move out, men," he hollered. There was a short, confusing spell when nobody budged. "'MOVE OUT,' I said!"

The Yanks scattered toward their bedrolls and equipment, which was piled at the side of the yard. In minutes they had loaded everything onto horses and wagons. They left straightaway, a choking cloud of dust following behind them as they headed southward.

Aunt Mariah turned to go up the porch steps but let out a squeal when the bushes next to her rustled.

Will climbed out of the thicket, pulling at the sack I saw him hide there, and stood with his bony chest puffed out like a rooster's. He grinned wide.

"Flour!" he said. "And there's more! Flour and coffee and—" He pulled the last of the three sacks from their hiding place and loosened the string on the last one. "—and salt! Hoo-eee! We're gonna have us some biscuits for supper, thanks be to them Yankee devils!"

Will's gladness gave me a chill, and for a short spell, I couldn't puzzle out just why. Then I saw the tiny print at the bottom of each sack: *United States Government Issue*, and suddenlike, it hit me. We'd both turned to thieving.

August 8, 1862, Mid-morning

Will and me sat on the porch steps at Winfrey. "I'm telling you," Will said, "there's books everywhere. All over Reverend Slaughter's lawn. Thousands of 'em! It was some wild Yanks what got in there. Tore that house apart!"

"Good thing the Reverend's stayin' in town," I said. "Something like that might've scared an old feller like him to death." I picked up the book Will'd brought as he moved off the steps and crouched in a sunny spot on the grass. He held his magnifying glass over an anthill.

"Mama know you was down to Slaughter's?" I asked. It was a far piece, and knowin' Mama didn't cotton to his roamin', I had to wonder.

Will glanced toward the open door. Inside, Aunt Mariah clattered dishes in the kitchen. "No, and don't you tell her," he said, low. "I heard Mr. Stofer say to Papa there's Confederate troops moving in from down that way. I's trying to find 'em."

"Did you?" I asked.

"Naw," he said, regretful. "Just books."

I nodded, thinking. "And they're outside, all them books?"

Will looked up from the magnifying glass. "'Course they're outside, Lonzo. I said 'on the lawn,' didn't I?"

"Was they nice as this one?" I asked, wagging the black leather-bound book in my hand. The gold lettering on the spine said *Oliver Twist*, and down a ways, DICKENS.

"Yep," Will said, and he went back to work, making the ring of sunlight under the glass smaller and brighter on the top of the anthill. The day was already hot as blazes, and the little soldier Ferdy'd carved slid around in my sweaty hand. I found a new scratch on its head and reckoned I ought to be more careful. I eased it back into my pocket, my stomach grumbling at the smell of baking biscuits floating out from the kitchen.

"Come on in now," Aunt Mariah called. When we sat down, big-eyed, to the first biscuits in a blue moon, she said, "Now remember, I've never tried my recipe with water instead of milk. We'll just have to see how they taste."

Dull and dry was how they tasted. But I didn't

mind it so much on account of how they made my belly full. Me and Will chewed quiet, taking big gulps of water between bites to ease 'em down. Aunt Mariah dunked hers in a bit of coffee, saying, "Mmmm!" now and again.

Will's magnifying glass sat atop the book he'd found, making the little gold drawing on the front a good deal bigger.

"You'll need to return this to Reverend Slaughter," Aunt Mariah said, tapping a finger on the book. "It's not right to keep it."

Will frowned. "But they was—"

"But nothing, young man," she said. "One person's evil deed does not justify another's. That's a good thing for both of you to remember."

"Yes, ma'am," we said together.

Will's shoulders slumped, and Aunt Mariah watched him over the rim of her coffee cup. "Well. I suppose you can hold on to the book until Reverend Slaughter comes back home." She sipped at her cup. "You take care of it proper, though."

Will grinned. "Yes, ma'am," he said. I saw how Will's smile was lookin' more growed up now, his teeth not too big for his face no more. It made my insides feel hollow, even with 'em full of biscuits. My brothers' and sisters' goings-on was s'posed to be familiar to me as my own body, but they was a mystery to me. When I came back, would little Ellen remember me?

Aunt Mariah poured some of the flour and salt and coffee Will had stole off the Yankees into her own tins, hiding them in the bottom of the potato bin. "We've got to get the rest of this to your mama and Weezie somehow," she said to Will. "But I can't let you take Big Moe. His foot's ailing."

"I can go and help carry, Aunt Mariah," I said. "And anyways, I ain't seen Mama or any of the young 'uns in two weeks."

I had another idea, too, on account of I could not get them books off my mind. How Ferdy would love 'em. And how they was sure to be ruined if they stayed outside on the Slaughters' lawn, where a good thunderstorm might come up anytime and give 'em a soaking.

The more I thought on it, the more the notion took hold in my head. The pleasure Ferdy'd get, having something new to read when he got home, even if he'd have to give 'em back one day. Ferdy'd done for me all my life, and I could not recall one single thing I'd done for him. And wouldn't Papa be proud of me when Reverend Slaughter told him I was a fine son! Yessir, rescuing some of them books would be a grand thing, and I meant to do it.

"Well, all right," Aunt Mariah said, patting my arm. "I suppose it'd do your Mama good to see you." I grinned. "But you'll have to go by way of the back fields. There might be Yankees anywhere along the roads."

We tied the sacks up good at the tops to make 'em easier to carry, and me and Will headed out across the fields. Will kept putting his sack down along the way to burn little holes in leaves and cornstalks with his glass. It was near 'bout more than I could tolerate till I came to see it was on account of the sack was too heavy for him. I was mighty happy when we finally came up to the back of our house.

Inside, I wasn't sure whether Mama was happier to see me or that coffee. She hugged me good, then said, "Weezie, can you believe it? Real coffee. Put the kettle on!"

Weezie gave me a big ol' squeeze and muttered, "Why, you're skinnier 'n a willow whip." Then she pulled away and grinned, her brown eyes shiny.

Mary Catherine, Abner, and even Tommy ran into the kitchen and hugged me about the legs. Little Ellen was too shy right at first, and I was thankful when she finally warmed up to me and giggled in my arms.

"Oh, thank heavens," Emma said, smoothing her hair in place as she came into the kitchen. I almost didn't know her. With her hair pulled back in a knot like Mama's, she looked all growed up.

"You take them awhile, Lonzo," Emma said. She pecked me on the cheek and went on upstairs, leaving me to stare after her.

I played on the floor with the young 'uns, letting

'em crawl all over me, then bouncing little Ellen on my knee while Mary Catherine fed me pretend tea from a tiny cup. Abner kept hollering, "Hyah!" and slapping the hindquarters of his rocking horse with a scrap of rope. I'd forgot what a noisy little thing he was.

When Mary Catherine brought me a book of nursery rhymes to read to her, I thought of Ferdy again, and how he was going to love all them new stories to read. A part of me wanted to jump up right then and run down to Reverend Slaughter's house, but there was another pulling, just as strong, to stay and love on my brothers and sisters. I did not know which way to go. I wanted to do them both.

A commotion outside sent Mama hurrying to the front door. She opened it just enough to poke her head out, then ducked in and shut it quick. "Union troops!" she said, going pale. "Heading south. Maybe a whole division!"

South. Toward Winfrey.

Mama looked at me, her eyes wide. They were the palest light blue, and it gave her the look of being smaller than she was, and breakable as a china doll. "Lonzo," she said, "you need to get back to Aunt Mariah."

"What about you and the young 'uns?" I asked.

"As soon as your papa hears, he'll come home," she said. "Don't you worry about us."

"Yes, ma'am." My heart sank. I had to leave my

family, and I could not get the books for Ferdy, either; the books would all be ruined.

Will came bounding down the stairs. "You ought to see 'em from our bedroom, Lonzo! It's a million of 'em, I bet! Maybe *two* million!"

"Oh!" Mama said, one hand flying to her mouth. "Grandma Nancy's candlesticks! Lord, I almost forgot. You have to take them, too, Lonzo."

"Candlesticks?" I said, confused.

Mama went to the closet floor and grabbed a pair of Papa's old boots. "Last time the troops came through, I barely got them covered with my skirt before Federals pushed their way past Weezie." She reached down inside each boot and pulled out a candlestick, silver and shining, and rushed to the kitchen.

Mama whirled about, panicky and red-faced. "I need something to bundle them in," she said to Weezie. Her fingertips lit on Weezie's great big apron hanging on a hook.

"Huh-uh," Weezie said, "you ain't taking my best apron, now." She pulled out Mama's big roaster and dumped the opened sack of coffee into it. "Here," she said, handing Mama the cloth sack. "Use this."

"Ain't they going to find them just as easy at Winfrey as they might here?" I said.

"Winfrey's a big place," Mama said, shoving one candlestick inside the sack. "Hide them under the hay in the barn."

Someone pounded on the front door. Weezie's black face turned ashy gray, but Mama moved fast, shoving the second candlestick into the sack and tucking it under my shirt.

"But Mama—"

"But nothing, Lonzo. These were your great-grandmother Nancy's. They're the only fine thing the Yankees haven't made off with, and I'll be damned if I'll let them take them!"

I stood gaping at Mama and her brave face. I'd never heard her swear before. The pounding came again at the door. The blue in Mama's eyes got icy and fierce. I knew then I couldn't tell her there wasn't no hay left in Aunt Mariah's barn to hide the candlesticks under, on account of Yankees takin' it for their own horses. Big Moe'd been grazing for his supper in the pasture since the hay had run out.

Mama hurried me to the back door and peeked out.

"We got to hide the food, too, Missus," Weezie called out in a panic.

Mama took in a sharp breath, then nodded, quicklike. "You go on, Lonzo," she said, turning me by the shoulders and pushing me outside. "We'll manage here."

I raced across the backyards along East Street, worrying about the troops at the door and where Mama and Weezie might hide the food and where I'd stow the candlesticks. At the south end of town,

I crossed a field and hunkered down low to spy on the road. Up ahead it split, part going southwest to Slaughter's Mountain, the other southeast to Stevensburg, right past Winfrey. The dry grass scratched at my arms and them candlesticks stuck me in the ribs while I watched and waited. Which way would the Yankees go?

Not two minutes later, they came 'round the bend, their swords blinding me in the sunlight as they marched. They turned toward Slaughter's Mountain.

I was relieved and mad as a hornet, all at once. Aunt Mariah'd be safe now, but what about them books? If the first mess of Yankees threw 'em outside, mightn't this bunch set 'em afire?

Right then, I knew what I had to do. I was faster'n any old marchin' Yankees, and if Ferdy's most favorite things in the world was waitin' for him, he would have to come back home. He would have to.

I took off to the south, tryin' as best I could to keep the woods or a house or a barn 'tween me and the Culpeper road where the Yanks was marchin'. I pretended Papa was timing me, *really* timing me, not just saying how he would and then not doin' it. My bare feet flew across dried-out grass and trampled wheat, and pounded on dirt that was hot and solid as an iron skillet. Sweat dripped off my face and ran down my back, and I clutched the sack under my shirt till my fingers cramped up.

My breath was coming in terrible gasps by the time I got to Slaughter's Mountain. I wondered if my aching legs could get me up the slope of the yard. I didn't see the books yet, but Reverend Slaughter's little chapel was all in ruins. Every window was broken, and small pieces of stained glass hung, sharp, from the window frames. *Damn Yankees!* I made my aching muscles work harder, and climbed.

Then, all a sudden, books was everywhere, like they'd rained down from heaven. The Yankees must've tossed some of 'em out the upstairs windows, they was flung so willy-nilly.

I pulled out the sack, leaving my shirt open on account of the heat, and commenced to gathering as many as I could. I shoved 'em in with the candlesticks, not mindful of titles a'tall, but trying not to pick the big heavy ones. I'd got the sack half full when I heard singing from down below.

There was Yankees coming up the lane! I scrambled about on my knees, shoving more books into the sack. It was dreadful heavy. I wrapped the opening round my fist two times and looked for somewheres to hide.

Beyond Reverend Slaughter's house and uphill some more was the woods. My legs already trembled from all the runnin' I'd done, and I knew they wouldn't hold out long enough to carry me all the way up there to hide. If I took the lane on the south side of the house, though, I'd be out in the open and easy to spot. But I didn't see as how I had a choice.

I started down the slope, hunkering low and dragging the sack behind me. At the bottom of the mountain, I hefted it over my shoulder and dashed 'round back of the Yeager place, then across the Flatgrounds road and into the woods on the other side.

When I'd got far enough into the trees to not be seen, I dropped to my knees, laying the sack aside and panting. Dry leaves crunched behind me, and I froze. My heart pounded and I shut my eyes. I was caught!

Nothing happened for a spell, and finally I turned. A squirrel clung to the tree behind me, his little white belly heaving with his breath. Then he scampered up the bark, scolding me with his chatter.

I took a long, deep inhale and blew the air out slow. Through the trees, I saw the sun starting its slide to the west. I had to get back to Winfrey. Aunt Mariah would worry with me being gone the whole day.

I set out, tramping along at a good pace but not running—my legs would not do it—and keeping the sun just over my left shoulder. I watched my feet plod along in the leaves and then the grass and then leaves again, wondering with every step what I'd say to Aunt Mariah 'bout taking all them books.

When I got to Cedar Run, I set the coffee sack down on the dry grass on the bank, rolled up the legs of my britches, and waded ankle deep. The cool water was a comfort to my feet, and I cupped my hands and drank. The water in the creeks was always better tasting than what came up from the well, like being outside made it come alive. I'd near 'bout got my fill when a long shadow fell across the water.

"What's in the sack, son?"

I jumped, choking, and fell backward with a splash.

The voice was deep, and the words came out how I'd never heard 'em said before. Quick, and pushed through somebody's nose.

Scrambling up, I turned to see a Yankee on the bank, close enough to spit in my eye. He pointed his rifle at the middle of my chest.

August 8, 1862, continued . . .

The Yankee was clean-shaved, no mustache or beard to hide the look of blame on his face. "Can't talk, eh?" he said.

I stood, dripping, in the shallows of Cedar Run, that rifle staring me down. Talk? I could not even breathe. *I'm caught. This skinny Yankee thinks it was me what stole their coffee and flour and salt! What is he going to do to me?*

He narrowed his eyes and stared me down, tilting his head a mite, taking in my rolled-up britches and my open shirt. "Why, you're just a boy," the Yankee said, lowering the rifle a hair. "You carry a knife?"

I thought of what was in my pockets: Grandpa's spyglass and Ferdy's carving. "No, sir," I said, shaking my head. "And I's fifteen last month."

The feller looked to be considering that for a

short spell, then crouched, laying the rifle at his side. "Fifteen. Well. You don't look too awful dangerous, even for a man of fifteen. Let's see what you've got in here," he said.

"*United States Government Issue*," he read off the bottom of the sack. He leaned in to sniff. "Coffee!" He threw me a shameful, scolding look and pulled out a few books. He set them aside, careful, on the grass. Then he brought out one of the candlesticks and let out a low whistle. "You steal these, too?"

"Oh, no, sir," I said, "them belonged to my great-grandma. You can't take 'em, you just *can't!*" I was mad at the pleading I heard in my words, but I had to make him see. "Mama sent me to hide 'em but I ain't got to it yet. She'll cry something awful if you take 'em! And I didn't steal the coffee, neither; that was my brother Will. But don't blame him; he don't mean no harm. He's just trying to be a man for Mama since I'm at Winfrey with Aunt Mariah, see? 'Cause Ferdy's gone off to fight and she don't have nobody else."

The words spilled out of me like they was water running to lower ground. Tears stung in my eyes, but I blinked 'em back.

The Yankee held up a book. "These belong to your great-grandma, too?" he asked, pursing his lips and looking doubtful.

"No, sir," I said. "Will told me they was up yonder at the Slaughters' place, all thrown about." Heat came up in my face then, and I felt a small measure of bravery. "It was *Yankees* what done *that*."

The Yankee in front of me raised his eyebrows.

"All them books was about to get ruined," I said, my fists clenching up, "and I had to save some of 'em for Ferdy, cause Ferdy loves books and would never throw 'em about like that. He's off fighting somewheres now, but if there's books like this waiting for him at home, I know he'll come back. He *will!*"

"Whoa, whoa, whoa!" the Yankee said. "Easy now."

There was nothing easy 'bout how I was feeling. My breath came raggedy and my blood boiled, thinking how that Yankee was so cocksure I was a bad feller. He did not even know me!

He turned the book on its side, running his long fingers over the fancy gold lettering. His eyes opened wide, and he grinned. "It's Longfellow!" he said, standing. "*The Courtship of Miles Standish*. This is a favorite of mine, written by a fellow from Boston. That's where I come from, Boston. Why—what's your name, young man?"

"Alonzo James Rosson, sir," I said, using a strong voice, but backing away a bit all the same. First he was pointing his rifle at me and calling me a liar, then happy as the day is long and friendly as my brother. I did not know what to expect next.

"Well, Alonzo James Rosson," he said. "Mr. Longfellow is quite famous in Boston, and I shall enjoy this book to no end." He gave a little chuckle, shaking his head like he still could not believe his good luck.

He crouched and gathered up the other books and the candlestick he'd laid out on the grass, and worked 'em back into the coffee sack. He propped the sack upright and set that book the Boston feller wrote atop it. Then, grabbing up his rifle, he stood.

He means to take away my treasures. What will I say to Mama? And how can I ever think of somethin' else as good as gettin' books for Ferdy? A choking sound came out of my throat, and I held back the tears that was building inside me.

The Yankee looked me over, taking his rifle into both hands. His face had got serious again, and I heard my heartbeat inside my ears. Was he going to shoot me?

Suddenlike, he adjusted the rifle to his shoulder and shoved a hand at me. "Lieutenant Robert Brandon," he said. "Pleased to make your acquaintance, Alonzo."

I did not know what to do. He had that rifle. I shook his hand and stepped back quick, my knees shaking.

When he let go of me, he tucked the special book under the arm what held his rifle, then gathered up the top of the sack and wrapped it round his fist the way I'd done. He picked it up. "Zounds!" he said, "What a weight!"

He set it down again, stared at it, and then walked in a circle all around it. "Alonzo, I don't believe I can carry that sack while I picket the road. I just don't believe I can do it." He looked at me, resting a fist over his puckered lips, one fingertip tap-tap-tapping on his nose. "You'll just have to carry it home," he said.

Then Lieutenant Brandon turned and marched off, the book in one hand and the barrel of his rifle sticking up over the other shoulder. Soon he was nothing but a black shadow, sunlit from behind. His outline looked exactly like the little soldier in my pocket.

August 9, 1862

I woke up in the gray of dawn. I was in Ferdy's bed, wearing nothing but my drawers. I sat up.

The Yanks was gone from Winfrey! I threw myself back on the mattress, spreading my arms and legs wide as I could, taking in the softness and smiling at a tiny crack in the ceiling. It looked just like Ferdy's crooked grin.

Then I remembered getting back to Winfrey last evening, and how Aunt Mariah was in such a tizzy. She'd cried and scolded and wagged her finger at me till I was sorry as I could be for making her worry.

But I did not tell her 'bout the Yankee feller. Instead, I showed her the candlesticks and said we should hide them in the privy, and I'd thought of that on account of that ratty little Custard and his knife.

Aunt Mariah laughed and rubbed my head. It was a marvel to see her happy again. She kept smiling right on through when I told her 'bout the books, making me promise I'd explain to Reverend Slaughter, first chance I got. Aunt Mariah knew better'n anybody how Ferdy'd love reading 'em, and that it was a good thing I done, saving 'em from ruin. We carried 'em into the parlor and lined 'em up pretty in the bookshelves.

Outside, Aunt Mariah helped me pound a nail in the underside of the privy board at the opposite end from the seat. When the nail was half-in, she gave it a whack sideways, making a nice hook. We hung the sack with Great-Grandma Nancy's fine candlesticks on it, just as dusk came on.

Now it was morning and I smelled coffee. I jumped up, my belly rumbling, pulled on my shirt and britches, and hurried down the stairs.

Aunt Mariah was staring out the back door when I got to the kitchen. "There's going to be a battle right over there," she said quiet, her voice quivering a mite. She pointed southwest toward Slaughter's Mountain.

I felt my smile drop away while I leaned to see 'tween the black walnut trees and the cedars that shaded the icehouse. Far off, a cloud of dust hung in front of the mountains to the south, and another blocked out the hills to the north. The rising sun threw streaks of rusty red across them.

"Pope's army," she said, pointing to the cloud on the right, "and Jackson's, I think," pointing left. She rubbed her fingers 'round the rim of her compass in smooth, slow circles.

"Aunt Mariah?" I said. "What if they come this way, fighting? What if they come *here?*"

Aunt Mariah turned away from the door and took a deep breath. "I don't know what'll happen, Lonzo. But God helps those who help themselves. We need to be prepared."

Tiny prickles ran up the back of my neck. *What does she mean, be prepared? Them soldiers have rifles!*

"Go wake Grandma and Grandpa," she said. "It's going to be a long day."

While we had our breakfast, we kept an eye on the dust clouds that inched closer and closer together.

Aunt Mariah wrapped the extra flapjacks she made in a towel and put them in a hamper, then set out collecting things from around the inn: water pitchers and cups, a stack of Grandma's quilts, books, letter-writing things, and two oil lamps. She sent me to the well for water, and I carried in two full pails.

"Take it all to the cellar," she said.

At noontime, we ate leftover cornbread and some beans from a jar. All four of us kept a watch out the back window, not saying much more than "pass that water pitcher" or "is there any more beans?"

The dust clouds had thinned and then disappeared altogether. What was happening at Slaughter's Mountain?

The early afternoon passed quiet while me and Aunt Mariah and Grandpa walked to and fro through the rooms, skittish as cats at any noise. Grandma rocked, her chair facing an east window, like she refused the notion that a battle might happen, and if it did, she didn't want no part of it.

It was still for so long, I got to hoping them armies had just tipped their hats and walked 'round each other, or mayhaps the men had sat down to read some books together on Reverend Slaughter's sloping lawn.

I knew that kind of wishing was foolish, though. Real things was never easy as a feller wanted 'em to be. Confederates was like Ferdy, stubborn, and the Yankees was mostly bloodthirsty. And everybody was sure they was right.

Tired of pacing about, I slid onto the bench at the kitchen table. I picked up the empty little pepper mill and turned the crank slow and unthinking, just listening to the scratchy sound of the stone inside. Aunt Mariah came and sat across from me.

"We're going to be all right," she said.

I looked up at her. "How can you know that, Aunt Mariah?" I asked. "I don't mean no disrespect, but how can you know that?"

Aunt Mariah sighed. "Have I ever told you the story of this compass, Lonzo?" she asked. She took it in her hand, rubbing the polished rim while the silver needle wobbled behind the glass, throwing tiny flashes of sunlight into her face.

"No, ma'am," I said. I knew it came from my dead Uncle John, who was Ferdy's papa, but that was all. I reckoned she wore it to remember him by.

"Well," she said, "your uncle John was handsome and charming and a wonderful person, but when he and I were courting, all he talked of, night and day, was becoming a soldier. He was like that when we were children, too—he was my cousin, you know, so I knew him from the time I was little. He read every book he could find about faraway places and adventure. When we got older, I hoped he'd outgrow wanting to be a soldier."

"He sounds like Ferdy," I said.

Aunt Mariah nodded. "Yes," she said, "Ferdy's very much like his father. That wanderlust was the only thing I didn't like about John. I was scared of losing him, you see. He was a marvelous rider and I had no doubts about his bravery, but I did not want to be left alone at home like an old maid while he traveled to God-knows-where. So I told him if he enlisted, we were finished.

"Well, your uncle John was persistent," she said, smiling soft. "For weeks he wrote me love letters and sang to me under my window at night. He'd wait at my door when it was time to walk to church or do the marketing. He didn't give up, no matter what I told him.

"Finally, he convinced me to marry him. I bought him this compass for a wedding present—"

"You bought it for *him?*" I said. "I thought—"

"Let me finish," Aunt Mariah said. "I bought him this compass for a wedding present, and when I gave it to him, I told him that if he wore it, he would never lose his way. It was my way of reminding him to come home." A tear ran down her cheek and dripped onto the faded blue calico of her dress, and I wondered if she was wishing she'd had a chance to give it to Ferdy 'fore he ran off.

"Well, after we married, he mustered in and was sent off straightaway to the Mexican War. He was wounded in the leg in the first battle, in Palo Alto, Texas. He said when he fell there was smoke everywhere and he'd lost his bearings. He couldn't see which way to crawl to safety.

"But he was wearing my compass, just like he'd promised. He pulled it out of his shirt and let the little needle balance, and crawled to the northeast, which was the direction back to Culpeper and me. It was all he could think of to do, since he didn't know the lay of the land. And it worked. His men found him, and he was furloughed to recover at home.

"He seemed to be healing nicely at first. But one day during the second week he was home, he started running a fever, and before we realized what was happening, he was deathly ill. That night while I sat with him he took my hand and pressed this compass into it. 'Mariah,' he told me, 'if you wear this compass, you'll never lose your way.'"

Aunt Mariah's face was wet with tears, but somewheres in the lines of her mouth and the little sparks in her eyes, I saw how she was still strong, through all what happened to her.

"So that's how I can know, Lonzo," she said. "Even with my husband dead and God sending me a baby to raise up all alone, I was all right. The truth is, I'll *always* be all right. Sometimes I just have to take a look at my compass and remind myself of where I'm going."

Aunt Mariah turned her face to the warm breeze coming through the window, and I watched a tiny fuzzy curl, moist from the midday heat, wave at her temple. Even after her story, I wasn't clear on how the compass helped her to know what all she said she knew. But I reckoned I would puzzle it out in time.

It was near on three in the afternoon by the parlor clock when the first far-off shell screamed through the air. Then came another and another, and in hardly any time a'tall, the countryside was loud with booms and shrieks. We could see the shells, dark streaks across the low sky, then smoke, beyond the hills. Sometimes little quiet spells came in between, but just as I let out my breath, there was more.

We helped Grandma down the steps, trying to keep most of the weight off her ankles, which was swelled up big as bedposts. Grandpa trailed behind, just a'cursing the Yankees.

On wooden chairs at the back of the cellar, we huddled together as if a howler storm was charging in to carry the house away. We heard the booms and rumbles and screams of rockets outside, muffled some through the surrounding earth and stone. At the same time, sunlight shot through the small window high on the west wall, its dusty bright streak lighting up a crate of empty canning jars on the shelf. It was like the world had lost its senses, sending us such fear on a pretty summer day.

Grandma trembled, and Aunt Mariah took her hand, patting it gentle.

I heard Big Moe scream from down in the barn, and I wanted to run to him and rub his neck and tell him "there now," but I couldn't. My chest squeezed up tight.

"Well, what are we going to do *now?*" Grandpa said over the noise. "Humph. I'll tell you what! Not a *dang* thing."

"Don't you go making everybody miserable now, Larkin," Grandma snapped. "Don't you dare!"

Grandpa rolled his eyes, the little clouds in the

middle of them turning upward while he scratched at his knees with yellowed fingernails.

"How about I read," I said. Grandpa'd liked when I read "Rip Van Winkle" a while back. Maybe it would settle his nerves.

A shell screamed, then exploded—ka-*boom!*—the sound swelling at the end like a train coming head-on. My heart raced.

I crouched to get one of the books Aunt Mariah'd picked out, then took my seat again, leaning forward. I read the title: *The Song of Hiawatha.* It was wrote by Longfellow, same as the book the Yankee kept for himself. I gulped, and trembling, stood to change it out for another one.

"An Indian story!" Grandpa said. "That'll do just fine. Sit down and let's get 'er started, Lonzo, or we'll all go crackers down here."

I swallowed to ease up the tightness in my throat, and with shaky hands, opened the book. I licked my finger, leafed past the introduction, and started in, picking across the words careful, on account of some of them being new:

On the Mountains of the Prairie,
On the Great Red Pipe-stone Quarry,
Git-che Man-i-to, the mighty,

That Indian name made me stop, but Aunt Mariah helped me out.

He the Master of Life, de-scending,

(Lord, another hard word. . . .)

On the red crags of the quarry
Stood erect, and called the nations,
Called the tribes of men together.

"It's a powwow!" Grandpa hollered out. "That's what he ought'a have called it. A powwow."

I stared at Grandpa. He blinked, staring back.

"Well, get on with it, boy. Read!"

I went on, feeling the sound of them words when I read across the lines. I'd never read nothing like *Hiawatha* before. The words was a drumbeat, so even and regular and steadying that even when the screeching artillery tried to shout me down, I kept on. Soon, them thundering booms in the distance was even farther away in my head. I read louder, feeling myself get more and more taken with Gitche Manito's words to them Indians with every verse:

Why then are you not con-ten-ted?
Why then will you hunt each other?
I am weary of your quar-rels,
Weary of your wars and bloodshed,
Weary of your prayers for ven-geance,
Of your wranglings and dis-sen-tions;

"Just slow down a bit. You're doing fine."

"Thank you, Aunt Mariah."

All your strength is in your union,
All your danger is in dis-cord;
Therefore be at peace hence-forward,
And as brothers live together.

I stopped for a short spell, turning them words over in my head. Walking backward over the lines, I looked for the part what I needed time on, and found it: *"Why then will you hunt each other?"* I swallowed hard. Them Indians was having a war, too.

The cellar dimmed, and I looked up. Gray smoke was rolling in around Winfrey like a sudden fog, blocking the sunlight that lit the room just a short spell before. A shell screamed at us, louder than any of 'em yet, and I saw the explosion bring a quick glow to the smoke. Tears streaked down Grandma's face.

"I think that's enough for now, Lonzo," Aunt Mariah said, biting her lip.

"Yes, ma'am." I marked the page with an old canning label and put the book aside. I would try to remember to go back to it later to see if them Indians stopped their squabbling, and how they done it.

Grandpa stared at the side window, jumping some with the crashing of cannon fire, and scratching his knees.

I lit one of the oil lamps and set it on an upturned crate. In the soft glow, I watched Aunt Mariah. She leaned forward now, her elbows resting in her lap while she held her compass, taut on its chain, in her fingers. She closed her eyes.

The basket of flapjacks sat on the tray next to a pitcher of water, but nobody touched 'em. The crashing and booming went on, the battle crawling closer like a terrible wild animal eating up the ground. The smoke was thicker at the side window, hiding the tall weeds at the edge of the garden. Soon an awful stink, something akin to rotten eggs, found its way through the closed window and the closed cellar doors and the solid stone of the walls.

As darkness fell around us, we pushed the chairs aside and padded the floor good with Grandma's old quilts. Aunt Mariah put out the lamp and we laid down, huddled on our sides against the back wall, each of us holding on to the one in front of us. I was farthest from the wall, so with nobody left to cling to, I clutched the edge of the top quilt. I couldn't see the squares good in the darkness, but I pretended like I had hold of Ferdy or Papa or Aunt Angelina and not just scraps of their worn-out clothes.

Something heavy plowed into the earth out-side—*whomp!*—and we felt its punch through the ground underneath us. Shells shrieked over the roof, exploding out front of Winfrey. Hoofbeats pounded somewheres in the back pastures, getting closer, then turning north. Big Moe screamed. Somebody hollered in the distance, scared and frightful shouts, but I couldn't make out the words. Then, some long minutes later into the madness and commotion, glass shattered on the floor above.

Grandma whimpered and Grandpa muttered curses. The hours dragged by. My muscles ached with cramps. Something stabbed at my right thigh, and my back itched where sweat had trickled down. I stayed in Aunt Mariah's clutches while the battering slowed and then quieted altogether.

None of us moved for a long time. A pale light came into the darkness of the cellar, building slow, like one tiny candle was lit, and then another, and another. At the side window, I saw the scraggly shapes of the tall weeds come clearer. In the moonlight, the smoke drifted off to the east.

It must've been near on midnight when we untangled ourselves and struggled to our feet, all wooden movements and hushed groans. Everybody but Grandma, who sat with her legs straight out in front of her on the quilts. "Is everyone all right?" Aunt Mariah asked.

I rubbed at the sore spot on my leg where I'd laid on Ferdy's carving, and rolled my neck. "I'm fine, Aunt Mariah," I said.

"I got to use the privy," Grandpa said.

In the dim light, I took him by the arm. "I'll go with you," I said.

I slid the bolt out of the hasp, climbed the first step, and pushed on the door, the hinge screeching like a barn owl in the quiet night. I let the door drop onto the ground, the air burning my nose and throat, and took another step up.

I gasped.

At the top of the stone steps and only an arm's length from the cellar door, a Yankee lay on his side in a dark puddle, his head lolling back and one outstretched hand clutching a dented canteen. His eyes stared, unblinking, at the stars.

August 10, 1862

I eased my back against the side wall of the cellar opening, quiet as a rabbit for a few long seconds. Was the Yankee still alive? I threw a look past Grandpa to Aunt Mariah and watched while she shook out a quilt, brought the corners together, folding it once and twice and a third time.

"Let's go, boy," Grandpa said and raised a foot, feeling for the steps, blind as anything to what lay right in front of him.

"Shh!" I told Grandpa, pulling gentle on his arm. I gathered up every bit of bravery in my soul and eased up one more step. Outside, the feller's rifle butt stuck out from under him. Both arms was in plain sight.

"Aunt Mariah?" I whispered.

"What is it, Lonzo?" she asked, pausing, another quilt draped across her arm.

"Come quick!" I said.

Aunt Mariah hiked up her skirt and climbed the steps, stopping short just as she got to the top. "Oh, Mercy!" she said. She scrambled out, grabbed the butt end of the rifle, and yanked it from under the Yankee. She tossed it clear.

Crouching down, she held one hand in front of his mouth, another to his neck. Then she drew a hand over his eyes, closing the lids. "He's dead," she said.

Grandpa tried to push me out of the way. "Dead?" he said, his voice tight and dry. "Who's dead?"

"It's a Yankee, Grandpa."

"Humph." Grandpa shifted from foot to foot. "A Yankee. Well, good riddance to bad rubbish. Now let me by. I need to use the privy."

I led Grandpa down the yard, guiding him 'round bloody, flattened places in the grass. My stomach soured, and for a short spell I wished my eyes was bad as Grandpa's. Being near 'bout blind allowed a feller to miss out on a heap of pain.

When we got back, Aunt Mariah'd already fetched the wheelbarrow, and she paced slow at the side of the yard. She stopped and looked across the lane what ran in front of Winfrey. "We've got to bury him," she said. "Maybe in the southeast corner of the wheat field, near that stand of trees. The wheat grows sparse there, anyway." Her voice was low but steady.

"Yes, ma'am," I said.

Aunt Mariah came to stand at the Yankee's head. "You know I'd do this on my own if I could, Lonzo, but I can't. Now, I'll get his arms and you get his legs," she said. Sweat shone on her forehead.

I swallowed hard and moved to the feller's dark boots. My breath came dry and choppy through my mouth. I'd never touched a dead man before.

It's just a Yankee, a damned old dead Yankee.

I took a deep breath, bent down, and with my eyes on Aunt Mariah, grabbed hold of his ankles. One hand touched skin instead of boot and I yanked away, shocked at the cold, damp feel. Aunt Mariah waited. I took hold again, and she slid her hands under his armpits. When she nodded, we lifted him together, gruntin' at his weight. His rump hit the rim of the wheelbarrow and we had to fight to get him into it, leavin' his legs to twist awkward and hang out. I pushed them 'round straight as I could, even knowing in my head it did not hurt him now to lie like that. His eyes eased open into thin slits, their whites shining blue in the moonlight. My stomach churned.

I dug the hole fast as I could with little breath and weak muscles. We lined up the wheelbarrow aside of it, then spilled the body into the grave and covered him up. I kept my eyes on the shrinking pile of dirt and not the growing one, till I was sure there wasn't nothing left to see of cloth or flesh.

Sweating, I leaned on the shovel. "I reckon we need to mark it so's it won't get plowed up," I said.

"You think you'll forget this spot, do you?" Aunt Mariah said, surprise in her tone.

I looked at her wide eyes in the moonlight. "No, ma'am, I won't," I said. "I won't *ever*. But what about when Ferdy and Uncle Jack and Uncle Edmund come home?"

Aunt Mariah's mouth came open a bit then. "Oh—oh yes," she said, "of course you're right, Lonzo. Of course." She started off to the edge of the woods. "Come help me find some rocks."

Soon as dawn broke, we got to work setting Winfrey to rights again. Aside from Yankee blood sinking into the dirt, she'd got off easy. There was two broken windows from a shell what must've missed the privy by a breath, a hole low in the barn wall, and a front section of the garden fence smashed away. The cannonball what done it was stuck in the ground a few yards out. There was other holes and ruts and gashes, too, and dirt everywhere it shouldn't ought to be, but none of it was worth fussing over. Even Big Moe came through, shaken up, but still breathing in and out.

Papa rode down to see how we made out through the battle. "I see the garden took a hit," he said directin' his remark at me. "Was that the worst of it?"

I wanted to tell him all about the dead Yankee, and how I had found him myself and helped to bury him, and that I was a man about it. But from where she stood behind Papa, Aunt Mariah put a finger to her lips and shook her head. *Be quiet.* I reckon she thought Papa did not need the worry.

"Yes, sir," I said, disappointed at not bein' allowed to tell. "That was the worst of it."

Papa grunted, then turned to Aunt Mariah and started in on how things was a mess in town with all the wounded, and how we should stay put at Winfrey till he let us know different.

Ten long days later, Papa came back, bringing Will and Tommy with him.

"There's goin' to be a parade!" Will hollered, jumpin' from the rickety flatbed wagon 'fore it came to a stop. It was early afternoon, hot as the dickens. "C'mon, Aunt Mariah! C'mon, Lonzo!"

While we got Grandma and Grandpa settled comfortable for the day, Papa told Aunt Mariah 'bout the armies burying their dead right in the Crittendon's cornfield next to Slaughter's Mountain, and how they even tore up Reverend Slaughter's chapel pews for coffins. I shuddered. I hoped I could find Reverend Slaughter in town and tell him 'bout his books. I wouldn't go out to his place ever again, if I could help it.

Tommy stood in the back of the wagon and yelled, "Hurry, we're gonna miss it!"

We climbed in and rode into Culpeper, Will and Tommy and me bumping and laughing and chucking one another on the arms all the way to town. My brothers was getting taller and stronger day by day. Every time I saw 'em, I missed bein' home more.

In town, I hurried into the house to hug Mama quick before we walked down to the parade. She was growing big in the middle with another young'un, and nobody had even told me. Maybe by the time she was ready to birth, I'd be home. I kissed her cheek and asked was she all right.

"Of course, Lonzo," she told me, "I'm just tired. Now get on out there. Your brothers are hollering like crazy fools!"

We hurried past the empty lots on Scanlon Street and over to Coleman. Before the crowds was even in sight, we heard folks a'hootin'.

People waved flags, and soon a great cheer went up. Pushing our way through, we saw raggedy columns of gray marching down the street, most of 'em barefoot. I grabbed hold of Aunt Mariah and pulled her with me to the front line, searching through that bobbing field of dirty faces and lingering on any one of 'em what favored Ferdy. How much would he have changed by now?

Suddenlike my breath caught in my throat. Billy

Colvin, who lived south of Winfrey just across the
Summerduck River, was there in the lines. "Billy!" I
hollered, choking in the dust. I let go of Aunt
Mariah and shoved past folks to stay even with him.

Billy turned his grimy face to me, then grinned,
his teeth looking whiter than snow on a blackbird.
"Hey there, Lonzo! How you been?"

"You seen Ferdy?" I yelled. My heart hammered
in my ears, and I ran sideways to keep up with the
column's pace.

Billy glanced this way and that at the crowd.
"No, is he here?" he hollered.

My feet went heavy then and I fell away. I kept
watching the faces in the columns, but knew, somehow, Ferdy was not there.

The days cooled and the leaves turned gold and red
and purple. The sun was rising later and setting earlier. There hadn't been any Yankees around for
more'n a month.

We dug up the food we'd buried in the woods and
saw it had some kind of little bugs in it. But we sift-
ed 'em out and ate it anyways. It was better than not
eating a'tall.

I raced up the lane toward Culpeper, pleased to
be on my way to get Tish after a quick stop at Papa's
store. I missed Tish almost as much as I missed
Ferdy.

But in town there was fresh talk of skirmishes along the Rappahannock and a second terrible battle up the tracks at Manassas—even bigger'n the one at Slaughter's Mountain—and my spirits fell hard to the ground. A wild jumble of feelings ran through Culpeper, some folks thinkin' we was winnin' the war, and others just as sure we was losin' it bad.

When I went into Papa's store, Old Mr. Saunders and Mr. Reed was playing checkers at the table and arguing. I said "Hey" to Will, who grinned and gave a wave as he unpacked some little something from a small wooden crate at the counter.

Then I went to Papa in the back room. "Mornin', Papa," I said. "I came to pick up some writin' paper for Aunt Mariah."

"Well then. You know where it is." He went on writing something in a little book.

"Yes, sir." I waited a long second, then said, "Things is fine at Winfrey, sir."

Papa looked overtop his glasses at me.

"We dug up the barrels," I said.

"Oh? And is the food edible?"

"Yes, sir. Just a few bugs, is all. We're doin' fine."

Papa nodded, watching me close. There was nothin' in his eyes to tell me what he was thinkin'. It might be *my boy's taken to eating bugs* or *what a wonderful son you've grown to be*. There was no way to tell, so I pretended he was thinking that last one.

From the front of the store, Mr. Reed shouted suddenly, "Pope don't know his headquarters from his hindquarters. Ol' Stonewall's stomping all over him."

"Hrrmph!" Mr. Saunders yelled back. "What rock you been hiding under, Elwon? It ain't even Pope anymore, it's McClellan. And Britain and France ain't going to help us out after all. Put *that* in your pipe and smoke it!"

"Well, I reckon that's on account of Britain's still mad 'bout that revolution," Mr. Reed said.

Mr. Saunders smacked his hand on the table hard, making both me and the checkers jump. "That ain't it a'tall!" he said. "More like, they ain't gettin' themselves mixed up with this slavery business."

"You mean to say the war's about slavery, do you?"

"I do," Mr. Saunders hollered.

"Well, I say it ain't no such thing." Mr. Reed pointed down at the checkerboard. "King me," he said.

Never mind who was *winning* the war, them two couldn't even puzzle out why we was having it! It made me feel a mite better at first, on account of they was grown-ups and in the dark as much as me. But soon I got to wondering: How could they hate somebody if they couldn't even work out *why*?

It scared me some, how I myself hated them Yankees. But 'least I knew exactly why. My life was full of hard edges and splinters now. They'd killed Sadie and roughed up Papa. They'd made Grandma and Grandpa sleep on the dirt floor in the cellar. I blamed 'em for Jacob getting killed and for Ferdy and my uncles being gone, and for Papa giving me away. Maybe that last thing wasn't the war's fault and would've happened anyhow; I wasn't sure. But I hated the Yankees, and I hated the war. I was tired of tryin' to work it all out, the right and wrong of it. I even hated the feel of that hate crawling around under my skin. And there wasn't nothing I could do about any of it.

I took a deep breath and collected Aunt Mariah's letter-writing paper, then left.

By the time I got to Uncle Daniel's I'd calmed myself, but a sour taste stayed on in my mouth. I waited for Tish on the front porch swing by the window, swayin' easy and watchin' leaves float down. Uncle Daniel and Aunt Angelina was fussing somewheres at the back of the house, their voices getting louder.

"But they're going to be free come January anyway, Daniel. Why *not* now?"

"No," Uncle Daniel snapped.

"We can send them up to Clara's in New York. All you have to do is sign the papers," Aunt Angelina said.

"I said no, Angelina! And that's the last I want to hear of it!"

"But Daniel, listen to reason—"

Smack!

"Papa," Tish's voice cried out, "leave her be!"

"Young lady, if you don't want to be next, you'd best hush!"

For a long second, panic gripped my chest and an awful silence fell over the house. Then I heard Aunt Angelina's soft sobs.

Like a streak of lightning, Tish came flying out the front door and across the yard, her hair wild in a gust of wind.

Clutching Aunt Mariah's package, I ran after her. Out on the road, I caught hold of her wrist.

"Let me go!" she screamed, wrenching her arm free and running harder.

"It's me, Tish! It's Lonzo," I called out. This time I touched her on the shoulder, not grabbing but laying my hand there while I ran alongside.

Tish stumbled and finally stopped, trembling all over. Her hands bunched into tight little fists. She stared at me, a mix of wildness and pain heaped in her eyes. "I hate him!" she cried through a tangle of yellow hair. "I hate my Papa!"

"No, Tish! No, you don't," I said. "It ain't hate—it's wrong to hate your papa!"

Tish sobbed into my shoulder.

"You're sore disappointed, is all," I said. "Sore disappointed."

June 10, 1863

Papa stood at the front door of Winfrey in the early dawn, hands clasped behind his back. A pale gray yellow glow, the color of a pine warbler's belly, seeped out from behind Mount Pony. I yawned.

Aunt Mariah and I had just been getting out of bed when he'd ridden up. "We're going to need you both in town today," he said, serious. "And one of you overnight as well. There's been a terrible battle." He lifted his hat to run a hand through his graying hair, then rubbed his eyes. "Our home's been converted to a hospital," he added.

Papa looked smaller than the picture of him I carried around in my head, all heavy-built and strong behind the counter in the store, gettin' folks whatever they needed, even when it seemed impossible.

Maybe I was just taller now; I was near on sixteen. Whatever it was, it gave me a chill.

"Where are the children?" Aunt Mariah asked.

"I've taken them all to the store and put Will in charge. There's no need for them to witness any of this."

I thought of poor Will, trying to look after Tommy and Mary Catherine, Abner and Ellen and our new baby, Robert Lee. I would not want that job all to myself. Robert Lee was five months old and he was a good baby, but that don't matter if there's four other busy young'uns to keep safe.

My papa nodded at the stairs. "Mama and Papa still asleep?"

Aunt Mariah nodded.

"Well, I suppose they'll have to fend for themselves for the day. Get them some breakfast and I'll settle them into the parlor. They ought to be all right if we put everything they'll need at arm's length."

All the way to town, I tried hard to hear what Papa was saying to Aunt Mariah, but his voice was low and the wagon creaked on the rutted road. The two hampers Aunt Mariah had packed bounced beside me on the flatbed, and I grabbed hold of the handles to keep 'em from sliding off.

When we turned onto East Street, Papa pulled the wagon to the side of the road. We wasn't even close to the house, but he looped the reins over a hitching post and said, "We've got to walk the rest of the way. There's no room for the wagon up the street."

I swallowed hard. What did that mean, no room for the wagon?

Papa and me lifted the hampers off the flatbed, and we all started toward the house. But the closer we got, the more I felt like I was in some awful dream. I squinted in the sunlight, bright now as it peeked between the houses. Soldiers lay about everywhere in the grass, bloody bandages and bloody uniforms, both blue and gray, hanging off 'em. Some sat propped against trees and up on folks' porches; some was smoking.

Horses, a few splattered with blood, was tied up everywheres and stinking to high heaven. Piles of manure crawled with flies.

We walked closer. Ambulance wagons lined the street, and medics dashed this way and that carrying the wounded. They hurried into houses at both sides of the street, then rushed off again towards the depot.

I saw our white fence up ahead and froze.

Papa turned and looked at me. "Come on, Lonzo," he said.

I made my feet move to the gate and stared at the house. With the sun in my eyes, everything in front of me was black and gray shadows. Bulky forms—

furniture?—was pushed to one end of the porch, with what could've been a rolled-up rug thrown on top.

Awful screams and moans came from inside, like the house itself was some huge, wounded animal, cryin' out. The stink, sour and bitter, turned my stomach.

I tore my eyes away and looked into the yard. I could make out pale rows of men on blankets lined up in front of the porch. Some of them writhed about, moaning; some was still. One lifted his arm from his side and made like he was trying to scratch under his chin, but I knew I wasn't seeing it right. His finger was too long and straight. One second later a shot exploded.

"Oh!" Aunt Mariah cried.

I turned, dropping the hamper, and emptied my stomach in the grass. That same awful blackness crept over me like the time I fainted when I had the chickenpox. *No!* I breathed deep, breath after breath, pushing light out to the edges of my vision again.

Aunt Mariah bent next to me, her hand on my shoulder, her own breath coming in little gasps. "Are you all right, Lonzo?" she asked.

I looked at Papa. His jaw clenched and let go.

"I'm fine," I said, pushing the words out from someplace deep, sounding strong as I could. I picked up the hamper again and started up the walk.

Inside the house, Mama, red-eyed and pale, hugged me and ran one hand down my cheek. Then she put me to work straight away, hauling pails of water, two by two, from the well out back. As soon as I put the fresh ones down in the dining room, one of the doctor's helpers—sometimes it was Aunt Mariah—threw in a bloody rag or a knife, dripping red.

Emma sat off to the side tearing bandages from sheets folks had brought. Her face was white as the cloth, her lips a powdery gray. She did not look up.

Back and forth I went. Every time I crossed the threshold into that room, I kept my eyes on the pails, on the floor, on the wall—anywhere but on them moaning soldiers, one after the other, atop the table. I looked out the window once, but there under it, and piled up almost to the sill, was arms and legs what had been cut off, some still wearing a boot, and flies all around.

I felt that hate rise up in me again, burning. I prayed silent prayers. *Make the Yankees pay, God.* But the burning didn't ease none with my praying. It got worse.

My legs was so tired I tripped at the top of the porch steps, spilling one of the pails. I watched the water seep through the boards and run down between the cracks. It felt like all the sweat I'd put into pumping it out of the ground and hauling it up the steps had disappeared into the dirt below.

I heard Papa's voice through the window. It was cracked and strained and so worn down, I wasn't even sure it was him at first. "I'll get them, Doc," he said. "Pete Hudson's got his men burying the dead ones, and I've got my wagon down at the corner, anyway. I'll get Alfred to help me. We'll leave the boots, though. Maybe we can match up a pair or two later on. So many going without . . ."

My breath caught in my chest. *Papa was going to bury them arms and legs.*

I shuddered and looked down at the water pail and the wet boards, seeing what a simple job mine was. In that minute, I loved my Papa and hated that war so much, I near 'bout couldn't stand it.

I took up the pails again and headed for the well.

When I came back in, Mama was waitin' for me in the kitchen. Her pretty brown hair hung loose on one side from its knot. Such a thing would've shamed Mama not very long ago. She was a proper woman.

"Put the pails down, Lonzo," she said. "There's something else I need you to do." She handed me writing paper and a pencil. "The men upstairs in the front rooms need letters written. They're being sent to the hospital or to jail in Richmond in a few days, and we need to let their families know they're alive."

I stared at her. Hospital or jail. Confederates or Yankees.

Mama stared back, her eyes red with weariness. "What if it were your uncles, or Ferdy up there?"

"Yes, ma'am," I said.

Upstairs, I opened the door to the bedroom I'd shared with my brothers back when I lived at home. Two fellers in their under-drawers was atop Will and Tommy's big bed, no sheet under 'em. Their gray uniforms lay over the footboard, dirt- and blood-splattered. One of the fellers had a big round bandage where his knee and the rest of his leg ought to be, and the other man, wrapped about the middle, moaned soft.

The feller in my bed was turned to the window, just the way I used to lie, watchin' the stars or the moon slide across the sky before I went to sleep. Seein' him there, I ached to be back home, to sleep in my own bed and hear a baby cry out in the night and then be quieted. All them things was real in that room, and it made me weak.

Then, while I stared at the feller's blue clothes, my hands commenced to shaking and I lost my breath. *The man in my bed was a Yankee.*

I stumbled back a step or two, grabbing hold of the flowery chair what sat beside the door, steadying myself and breathing deep.

Weezie came up behind me. "Everythin' all right in here?" she asked.

I looked at her, anger rising to my throat, then over at the Yankee in my bed.

"You goin' to take care o' writin' some letters, ain't you," Weezie said. "You're going to do what you was told, ain't you." She watched me, and I knew them things she said wasn't questions. She laid a hand on my shoulder, nodded toward the beds, then went into Mama and Papa's room and shut the door.

I made myself go to the big bed and say, "I'm sent to write to your folks, if you want."

"That'd be mighty kind," the feller with the missing leg said, his voice weak.

I pulled the chair to the table between the beds, and setting the paper on it, I took down what he said for his mama and daddy in Alabama.

It ought to have made me glad, doing the soldier that favor. But I wasn't glad. Something gnawed at me, something I couldn't name.

When I finished, I turned to the other feller. He wanted me to tell his sister in North Carolina he was alive. He told me the town.

"How's that spelled?" I asked. When he didn't answer fast enough, I said, "Tell me the letters!" My words snapped in the air like icy twigs.

"R-A-L-E-I-G-H," he said, slow. I wrote it all out, pressing hard with the pencil, till the words screamed from the page, mean. I hated how it felt to write them, and how they looked on the paper. But I could not make them any other way. I stood, putting them two papers to the bottom of the pile, and went to the foot of my own bed.

The Yankee rolled over, slow, to face me. "My turn?" he asked.

I near 'bout fell over. His cheek was scraped up on one side, and a dark stubble of whiskers grew on his face, but there was no mistakin' him. "Lieutenant Brandon!"

"You remember me," he said, smiling, then wincing, as he lifted his bandaged right arm to rest on his belly. He still wore his full uniform, all but the sleeve of his jacket, which was cut away at the shoulder. His right hand was gone.

I stood numb, root to branch.

"I need a letter, too. I won't be writing my own for a while." He lifted his left hand. "At least until I learn to do it left-handed."

I pulled the chair over and fumbled with the stack of paper in my hand, holding it, clumsy, on my knee. My fingers went to pins and needles, but I kept on taking my breath in deep. I touched the tip of the pencil to my tongue, fixing to write.

Lieutenant Brandon frowned. "Here," he said, struggling for something inside his jacket. He brought out a little book. "Lean on this. It's easier to write that way."

The Courtship of Miles Standish. I stared at the little gold letters on the spine, remembering when he took the book from me in the woods. I settled it under the paper on my lap and waited.

"The letter's to my son, Robert," Lieutenant

Brandon said, "but we call him Robbie. Named him after me. Firstborn and all that, you know." Sweat ran down the side of Lieutenant Brandon's face, and his words came slow. "He's ten. Loves to play Rounders. Do you ever play Rounders?"

I shook my head. I did not even know that game.

"Well," he said, wincing a bit. He glanced down where his right hand should've been. "Guess I'll need to learn to throw left-handed, too," he said.

I tried to swallow, but couldn't.

"We'd better get started," he said. " Let me know if you need help with the spelling, Alonzo. I'll go slowly. Ready?"

I nodded.

"Dear Robbie," Lieutenant Brandon said. *"I'm coming home. But I wanted to tell you first that I've been wounded. I suppose you'll be mad, knowing someone hurt me. But being mad won't get my hand back."*

Lieutenant Brandon's voice had got soft while he talked, just like he saw his boy in front of him and was spelling out how things was, easy and gentle.

"I heard a story I want to tell you before I come home, Robbie. Maybe you've heard it before. But even if you have, I want to tell you of it again. It goes like this: An old Cherokee was teaching his grandchildren about life. He said, 'There is a terrible fight raging inside me. It is a fight between two wolves. One is evil; he is greedy and stingy and a liar, and he lives by fear and anger.'"

Lieutenant Brandon waited for me to catch up.

"'The other wolf is good; he is generous and honest, kind and peaceful and forgiving. This same fight,' the Indian told his grandchildren, 'is going on inside you, every day.'

"The children thought about it, and finally one child asked, 'Grandfather, which wolf will win?'"

"The grandfather answered, 'The one you feed, little one. The one you feed.'

"Think about this story, Robbie, and we'll talk about it when I get home. Love, Papa."

I looked up at Lieutenant Brandon. "Feed the good wolf," he said.

The lump had closed up my throat worse than before and I could not talk. But my head was full of one thing: I did not want to feed *either* wolf.

November 16, 1863

I heard him 'fore I saw him, his bawl echoing off the sides of the Deep Cut in the sharp morning wind. A trapped critter, I reckoned. I stretched out my stride from four rail ties to five, weighing up in my head what sort of creature might put on such a howling. I hoped he wasn't too awful big. In the Deep Cut, there wasn't but two ways out—back the way I'd come, and past whatever it was. But the thing's wail set my teeth to aching and I was sorry for its pain. *Please, God, don't let him be so bad injured he can't run off when I set him free.*

When I rounded the bend in the tracks, a wicked chill shot through me. My steps slowed till I stood still, panting and hugging Uncle Jack's old jacket tighter 'round my belly. My feet felt like they was mired in mud and then froze there, they was so heavy.

The thing up ahead was a *man*—a sobbing ghost of a man, surely, but a man all the same. He came at me in a peculiar rocking sort of walk, head down, like his feet wasn't apt to move along on their own lest his eyes told 'em to. His soldier cap looked too big for the rest of him.

The sight of a bedraggled fighting man wasn't a new thing in this neck of the woods; they was common for months at a time and then scarce, ebbing and flowing like the tides. But it wasn't a common thing for one to be bawling, 'specially without a crutch or an empty sleeve.

Both this feller's legs was still attached, and both arms, too. All the same, he looked to be missing something. His gray britches and jacket hung loose about his bones, and a long strip of cloth trailed from one foot like a trampled flag.

He came closer, making a ruckus and pushing one foot ahead of the other. Now and again, he wiped his scraggly-bearded face with his sleeve. Finally, he looked up and saw me, and stopped. Then, slow and careful, he backed up a mite. He looked side to side, like maybe for someplace to run. But there wasn't none, just two high walls of rock, dotted with scraggly brush.

His bawling quieted down to just sniffly, scared whimpers whilst we stared across the distance at each other. The cloth at his foot lifted and lowered in the wind, up and down, up and down, like a ghost too tired to float about. The man cocked his head sideways, his face lost in the shadow under the tattered cap.

"You all right, feller?" I called out.

He jumped back like my words was bullets, his arms raised, one a good bit higher than the other. But then, with a sudden gush of strength, he started running at me! His hat fell off and I saw his head was wound up in a cloth, just like his foot, with a streak of rusty brown straight across the top. He ran like he walked, pitching side to side and forward all at once.

Oh, mercy, a crazy man!

Then it was *me* thinking 'bout running. I edged to the side of the tracks to let him blow on past if he had a mind to, and braced myself in case he was fixing to bring me down. I didn't reckon it would hurt me none, skinny as he was, but it didn't seem right somehow to run away from him, neither. He was wounded, and likely out of his mind with pain.

I covered my eyes with both hands and held my breath. Then, flattened against the rock, I peeked 'tween my fingers. My hands dropped to my sides, fingertips a'tingle, and my knees near gave out under me.

"Ferdy!"

I fell into him, huggin' and dancin' him around, pullin' back to make sure it was really him, then squeezin' him some more. "You're alive! You're alive and you're home and you even got arms an' legs!" I near busted wide open with happiness.

Everything would change now. Aunt Mariah would go back to singin', and the years would drop off Mama's face, and Papa might even smile now and again. Yessir, everything was going to be fine. I hugged Ferdy some more and jumped about, knowing if I didn't, I might explode—*pow!*—like the cork off a jug of ripe cider. Ferdy didn't say nothing, but fresh tears dripped off his chin, and he smiled his crooked smile, just like I remembered.

"Does your head hurt?" I asked.

Ferdy commenced to crying again, crying too hard to talk. But he smiled through them sobs, and I reckoned the pain wasn't so bad.

I took him by the arm—*oh, praise the Lord, he had arms!*—and turned back the way I'd come, toward Winfrey. "Well, your mama can change that dressing for you soon's we get you home. Oh, Ferdy, won't we surprise her! I was s'posed to be going to Papa's store for her right this minute, but if'n I bring back you 'stead of cornmeal, what do you bet she won't throw no shoe at me!" I laughed, and Ferdy kept on crying.

"She ain't done no shoe-throwin' since you been gone, Ferdy, but she threw a spoon at me once. And she threw hams at the Yanks! *Hams*, Ferdy! That was something I wish you'd'a seen! I thought she took leave of her senses." The words spilled out of my mouth like I was a magpie gone to heaven. I could not stop.

"You're going to be surprised how Winfrey looks, too, Ferdy, but don't you worry none. I tried to keep up the fences 'round the pastures when you first was gone, but it just ain't no use anymore. Yanks use 'em for firewood soon as I get one little section up.

"It's going to be different now, though, ain't it?" I said. "I bet Uncle Edmund and Uncle Jack are right behind you, and soon we'll have us a mighty celebration, we will!"

I talked nineteen to the dozen all the way to Winfrey, circling Ferdy and walking backward in front of him and sometimes skipping. I saw now how both Ferdy's feet was wrapped in cloth 'cause he was lacking shoes; the darker cloth was just tied better'n the other.

I told him about Sadie and how brave Aunt Mariah was, and how we fought back all we could those first times the soldiers came through. Ferdy stopped his blubbering and looked to be listening good while I talked.

'Fore I knew it, we was coming up Winfrey's porch steps. Ferdy stopped in front of the door and looked at me, his eyes red-rimmed but blue as a patch of spring larkspur.

"Go on," I said, quietlike. "Go see your mama."

I clomped after him, his padded feet quiet as a house cat's on the floorboards. The *whoosh-swoosh-whoosh-swoosh* of laundry being scrubbed on the washboard led us nearly to the kitchen 'fore it stopped and Aunt Mariah called out.

She must've thought we was a traveler coming in. "I'll be right with you," she said, her stooped back toward us as we came to the doorway. "I didn't hear your horse!"

I saw the worry on Ferdy's face. "Go on," I said, giving him an easy push.

"Lonzo?" Aunt Mariah turned, then froze, a block of lye soap dripping in her hand. Shiny streaks lined the sides of her face where the sweat had run down, leaving dark spots on her dress. All at once, she gasped and dropped the soap and rushed forward, scaring the teewaddy out of me. Ferdy flinched as she came at him, but she stopped short of slamming him to the wall, and instead, wrapped him up with easy hugs and streaming tears and gentle pats round about his face. "You're hurt," she cried, "oh, you're *hurt!*"

"Lonzo," she said, getting taller right before my eyes, "see Ferdy to the bedroom while I get fresh dressings. And try to find a bedsheet!" Turning back to Ferdy she said, "I'll bet you're hungry, son. Are you hungry?" She patted at his face some more and waited. When Ferdy still didn't answer, a quick look of fright flashed in her eyes. "Well, of course you are," she said. "Go on up, and I'll bring something in just a minute." She gave us both a nudge and busied herself pulling tins out of the cupboard, setting the empty ones aside. "The boy's hungry, that's all. He's hungry as he can be."

A bad feeling came to my stomach then, a sour, sick feeling. I walked with Ferdy through the hall, the front room, and up the steps, watching him sideways. Tears leaked out of his eyes again, but not one single word came from his mouth. He hadn't said nothing since I found him caterwauling on the railroad tracks. Nothing a'tall.

November 16, 1863,
continued . . .

"Here, Ferdy," Aunt Mariah said, patting the quilt atop the bed. "Come sit and let me take a look under that bandage."

Ferdy sat in the side chair, his damp face wearing a befuddled look.

"Come now, I'll do my best not to hurt you," Aunt Mariah said, nervouslike, as she smoothed the bandages she'd cut from Grandma's quilting muslin. Her mouth stretched into a tight smile.

Ferdy still did not move.

Aunt Mariah took hold of his arm, led him to the bed, and pressed him down, gentlelike. "That's better," she said. Her trembling hands unwrapped the dirty cloth.

There was no telling how old the blood on the bandage was. Underneath, a furrow, crusted over and dry, was dug across the top of Ferdy's head. It was wide as my pointer finger, and almost as long. My own head ached seeing it, and my knees near gave way. I sat in the side chair to steady myself.

"Mercy," Aunt Mariah said, slow tears coming down her cheeks again. She wiped them away with the back of her hand. "Ferdy," she said, her voice a whisper in that quiet room, "tell me what you remember, son."

Ferdy watched her lips move, and I saw him look from her mouth to her eyes and back again.

Aunt Mariah waited.

"He probably don't remember anything, Aunt Mariah," I said for Ferdy. "I reckon he'd rather not think about that, anyway."

Aunt Mariah glanced at me, then looked back at Ferdy, lifting a damp cloth to his head and stroking it, easy. "Where were you, son? Can you tell me that?"

"He's been all over, it looks like, Aunt Mariah." I rubbed my sweaty hands on my britches. "Wore the shoes clear off his feet. I reckon he's awful tired, too."

Aunt Mariah quit wiping at Ferdy's head and turned to me.

I saw something fierce in her eyes. "Lonzo," she said, "Thank you for your help. Please go into town and tell the family Ferdy's home." Her words had changed over, somehow, in that short spell at the bed. There were sharp edges and cut-off ends, and hearing them gave me a chill.

I stood up, voiceless as Ferdy, and put my coat on. When I got to the lane, I set out runnin'. At first I couldn't go very fast. But soon my feet pounded angry on the road. I could feel the sobs buildin' inside me, twistin' knots in my chest and my throat, chokin' me in their fight to get out. I flew around the bend in the Deep Cut, gaspin' in the wintry air. When I got to the place where I'd found Ferdy, my legs gave out under me, all their strength gone. I dropped to my knees on the tracks and began to howl.

I knelt there, wailin', till my voice got cracked and broken. Then, while the muffled echoes of my sobs came back at me from the rocky walls, I heard it in my head: I sounded just like Ferdy. The notion gave me a shock. Ferdy, who'd always been strong and brave for me, had changed. It was him that needed somebody now.

I rose up, wiping the cold tears from my face, and looked ahead to the straight path of rails. All the time Ferdy'd been gone, I'd been waiting for him to come back and take charge of things again, point out the direction we'd go, decide what needed doing first. But now it was clear that he could not do it. I started running again.

Every step toward town made me stronger. I found Papa standing at the counter in the store, his fingertips to his forehead, holding a piece of paper. I told him straight out, "Ferdy's home, Papa, but there's something wrong with him. He's been shot across his head, and he can't talk. 'Least he hasn't yet."

Papa looked me in the eye, and for the first time in my sixteen years, I did not shrink in my skin when he did it. "I see," he said in a quiet voice.

"I'll go tell Uncle Daniel, sir."

Papa's brow wrinkled a bit, and he gave me a queer look. "Never mind that, Lonzo. I'll send Will." Papa glanced to the back of the store, then folded the paper and tucked it inside his vest pocket. "And I'll go back to Winfrey with you," he said. "I've got to talk with your Aunt Mariah."

Papa was quiet on the ride out to Winfrey. We found Aunt Mariah and Ferdy in the kitchen, an oil lamp on the wall glowing soft on their blank faces. Ferdy, a new muslin bandage wrapped about his head, sat at the table. With long, slow strokes, he rubbed his fingers back and forth, tracing out the grain of the wood.

"He wouldn't stay in bed," Aunt Mariah said. Facing us, the shadowy light made her eyes and mouth look hollow, like they was just holes in her head.

I went to sit with Ferdy. When he looked up at me, I saw shiny tracks on his cheeks where his eyes'd leaked some more. He smiled his crooked smile while I patted his hand and tried to smile back.

Papa went to Aunt Mariah and took her by the shoulders. "Mariah," he said, his voice cracking. "It's—"

"I'm okay, Bernard. I'm fine," she said. But there was no feeling in her words, nothing warm to make anybody believe them.

"You don't understand," Papa said, his voice shaky and thin. He let loose of her shoulders and slowlike drew out the paper I'd seen him reading in the store. "It's Edmund and Jack," he said. "They're not in the Federal's prison like we thought. They were killed last year, back when they took the fort. There was a mistake, an awful mistake with the records. Nobody knew till now."

All at once I couldn't breathe and my skin went prickly. I remembered Aunt Mariah at her writing desk, looking out the window from time to time and wearing that quiet smile. I knew she'd been thinking what she might say to her brothers to make their wait to the war's end easier. A sharp pain stabbed my chest.

All that time, Aunt Mariah'd been writing to ghosts.

Papa pulled her close, and I saw his face soften and crumple and his shoulders shake. He broke down in big gushing sobs. Aunt Mariah stood straight and stiff in his arms, all hardness and chill. In the sidelong glow of the lamp, I saw her jaw clench and let go, clench and let go.

It got hard to breathe then, and I had to think about takin' the air in and lettin' it out again.

Everything was overturned and battered, like a storm had plowed through my family. I grabbed the sides of the table, afraid somehow that if I didn't hold on to something firm and heavy, I'd just fall, and keep on fallin' forever.

Late November, 1863

Yanks was wintering in Culpeper, making themselves at home in houses and hotels all around. They filled every bed at Winfrey, plus the floors in the parlor and the tavern room. They stayed up late at night playing card games and sometimes taking in corn whiskey from a flask, all our liquor being gone. Then they laid all over the floors till way past dawn.

Aunt Mariah had pleaded with the Yankees for a bedroom for Grandma and Grandpa when winter set in, but the soldiers broke their promise good and quick when a terrible cold snap hit. Grandma and Grandpa was sleeping in the cellar again. Me and Ferdy and Aunt Mariah crowded onto the kitchen floor, where the men who'd drunk too much stumbled over us on their way to the privy through the night.

So far this morning, the Federals was all still asleep. Ferdy and me had just finished our breakfasts and Aunt Mariah was washing up our bowls, when all a sudden, Ferdy jumped off his chair and ran out the door into the bitter cold with no coat or gloves or hat.

"Ferdy, wait!" I called, and ran after him. I tried to pull him back to the house, but there wasn't a workhorse in the county strong enough to do that. "Where you goin'? You got to wear a coat or you'll catch your death," I said.

Ferdy shrugged me off, not shiverin' or huggin' his arms like I was, just crying soft. Seemed like his body was numb, leaving his heart to feel every painful thing there was.

I followed behind him till he got what he was after, which was a chunk of broken branch at the edge of the woods. He headed straight for the house then, and when we got inside, for the paring knife in the kitchen drawer.

"No!" I said, grabbing his hand away as he reached for it. I was scared to let him have a thing so sharp. He could not even button his shirt with them fingers. What might happen when he got hold of a knife?

Ferdy stomped his foot and cried and pounded his fist on top of the dry sink while I blocked the drawer and Aunt Mariah stared at us both.

Finally Aunt Mariah came over, took the knife from the drawer, and put it down in front of Ferdy. "Let him have it," she said and walked away.

I held my breath, watching what Ferdy'd do. He sat at the table and turned the hunk of wood over and around in them big cupped hands of his, tears still dripping off his chin. Then, ever-so-gentle, he stroked the blade of the knife along a rough edge once, and again, and again. His moves was not quick like before when he whittled, but measured and thoughtful, like he already loved what might come out of the wood.

Five days before Christmas, I came in with the water pails soon after daybreak, the kitchen still, as it had come to be in the last month, 'cept for the low grating sound Aunt Mariah's spoon made in the pot on the stove.

Ferdy sat quiet at the table, carving. I set the pails near to the stove and rubbed my froze hands. With Ferdy's silence and Aunt Mariah all shut down, I was lonesome as anything.

"What're you fixin' to carve, Ferdy?" I asked. I didn't count on getting an answer; I only needed to hear some words floating about, and my own was better than none.

Ferdy held up the smooth, knobby shape he'd been working at. He ran his hand over it like he was petting a cat. But the piece was nothing like a cat. When I looked close, I could tell it was s'posed to be a bird. There was a little beak and some feather markings, but they was all rounded over like a baby's toy. A bird like that could never fly, not with them fat wings and tail feathers. Ferdy'd finished a whole row of them rounded-off animals—squirrels and groundhogs and such—which would not stand proper, only rock, and lined 'em up on the window ledge.

"Ferdy, you got to give 'em some sharpness and edges, or they ain't real," I said. I held up the little soldier carving he'd made, so he'd see what I was saying.

He looked at me peculiar. I walked backward through my words and then saw why. My wanting sharpness was a new thing for him.

The stirring at the stove stopped. "Lonzo," Aunt Mariah said, her voice low, "we're going to services this morning." She nodded to some folded-up clothes on one of the chairs. "There's some clean drawers and britches for you and Ferdy. Get yourselves dressed."

Services! We had not been to church in a month. I reckoned Aunt Mariah'd given up on God after He let her brothers die and stole her boy's words. But we was going to services! Was she giving God another chance?

"Yes, ma'am," I said, happy to see this change in her.

I took up the clothes and dressed quick, then helped Ferdy, holding open the leg holes of his long handle drawers till he pushed one foot and the other into 'em. We did the same with his arms in the sleeves. I handed him his trousers and he put 'em on his own self, and when he was buttoned-up proper, I looked him over. He was fit to be seen but for his hair, which stuck up every which way around that gash in his head. The scab was gone now, but not a lick of new hair grew on the worm-pink wound. I spit on my hand and rubbed the wild hairs on either side down gentlelike, covering the scar best I could.

Aunt Mariah set two bowls of cornmeal grits on the table. "Eat your breakfast," she said. "And when you're finished, take this tray down to Grandma and Grandpa."

"Yes, ma'am," I said.

While I started in on my grits, Aunt Mariah pulled tins from the shelves and crockery from a low cabinet. The little silver compass what Ferdy's daddy gave her clanged into the cabinet door and she pulled it over her head with a quick yank, setting it aside.

When she laid that compass down, I noticed what all she had pulled out. Flour, lard, and milk. There wasn't salt anywheres, but Will had brought the flour and milk yesterday, hiding the milk in a canteen under his coat.

"Aunt Mariah," I said, excited, "we having bis-cuits, too?" We had not had biscuits for a blue moon on account of no milk. For the last month, the Yanks in town had kept the little milk there was for their own. There was no telling what Papa'd done to get that full canteen for us.

Aunt Mariah was coming back to her old self! We would eat our biscuits and go to church, and she would make up with God. Things was going to be better, sure as the sun kept on rising over Mount Pony.

Aunt Mariah turned to me quick. "No, Lonzo," she said, "we're not having biscuits."

What I saw was the makings for biscuits, I was sure. "But Aunt Mariah—"

"Our Yankee guests are having biscuits, Lonzo," she said, quick and breathless. "Now hurry down-stairs with this tray."

She picked it up and pushed it at me, two bowls of cornmeal grits and cups of sweet potato coffee.

I took the tray and carried it toward the cellar steps. The Yankees? She was making her special biscuits for the *Yankees*? Stopping at the top of the cellar steps, I looked back and stared.

"Go on," she said, her voice edgy, her fluttery hands waving me away.

I carried the tray down the steps, my face burn-ing. *Making biscuits for the Yankees!*

I woke Grandpa and draped a quilt around his

skinny shoulders. Then, carrying Grandma's chamber pot, I pulled Grandpa up the cellar steps outside and through the cold to the privy. I was so riled about the biscuits, I hardly felt the chill of those minutes my own self.

When we got back to the cellar, Grandpa lay down again. "I'll wait and eat when Miss Polly wakes up," he whispered.

I nodded, still fuming, and started up the stairs. *I'll tell Aunt Mariah it ain't fair. That milk was for us, not the damn Yankees. Them biscuits are ours!*

But when I got to the top step, I froze. I watched Aunt Mariah pull a tiny sack, the one with them empty, evil skull's eyes on it, off the top shelf.

Rat poison. People poison, too.

Aunt Mariah opened it as I stared from across the room. Powder fell into the bowl. A handful, white and still. She closed the package, put it up again. Her wooden spoon slapped quick and mean on the crockery.

A terrible buzzing filled my ears and my mouth dried up, choking me. I coughed.

Aunt Mariah jumped, knocking her compass to the floor. "I didn't hear you," she said. Her eyes were on the spoonfuls of dough she piled on the baking pan, like she was talking to them and not me. She moved about in a rush, kicking the compass aside with her hard little Sunday shoe, and slid the pan into the top oven. She threw the spoon in the fire below. "That spoon was starting to splinter," she lied, looking at me sideways, then put up the tins and wiped her worktable clean.

I swallowed hard and turned to Ferdy, like I used to do when I was lost on things. But Ferdy was lost, too.

I crossed the room, picked up Aunt Mariah's compass from where it'd fallen on the floor, and sat across from Ferdy. I lifted and lowered the silver chain again and again, letting it puddle into my palm.

When the biscuits were done, Aunt Mariah took them out and piled them on a plate. She draped a towel over them, opened up the pass-through to the tavern room, and hushed as a ghost, set them on the sill.

A prickly feel came to my hands. I wiped specks of flour from the back of the compass, and turning it over, saw the shattered glass and the bent needle. Aunt Mariah's compass had broke.

December 20, 1863, 8:30 A.M.

Aunt Mariah put on her coat and Sunday hat, leaving me to help Ferdy. She hustled us quiet out the back door. With her Bible under one arm and a quick look back at Winfrey, she set a fast pace toward town. I took Ferdy's arm to pull him along, but every step my own feet made away from that inn was more of a chore than the last.

Aunt Mariah stared straight ahead while me and Ferdy struggled to keep up. She didn't seem to take note of the Union lookout atop Mount Pony, or the encampments here and there spilling Yankees near 'bout into our path. She marched on, her head high, like they wasn't there, and there wasn't no war, and them poisoned biscuits did not sit on her bar at Winfrey.

Horses and foot soldiers had roughened the pastures into a curd of raw earth and dead grass. Here and again, deep gashes marked the soil, great open wounds in the earth where cannonballs was stuck fast in icy clay. Not a fence was left anywhere, and the edges of every wooded piece of land showed jagged stumps where trees used to be. There was no cows or hogs or chickens, and thick branches of the apple trees in Jameson's orchard was hacked off like shot-up arms.

We hurried down East Street, past the wrecked buildings near the Episcopal church, past smashed headstones in the cemetery where even the dead was not left in peace.

Farther down the road, inside the little Methodist church my family went to, I was relieved to see it was the same as last time I came. The pews was still there, not made into coffins like at Reverend Slaughter's chapel. Mama and Papa and my brothers and sisters was seated in their usual spots. Tish waved to me and Ferdy from two rows up.

But by the time services started, I was seeing what wasn't there more than what was. Everywhere I looked, there was missing arms, missing legs, missing uncles.

I stood and held the hymnal Mama handed me so Ferdy could see it, too, even though I knew he would not sing. I felt the throbbing notes of the organ through my feet. All around us, mouths opened and closed. But neither me nor Ferdy sang with the rest, "O come, all ye faithful."

I could not feel my hands or my face. The room turned slow around me, and I tried to rest my eyes on Tommy, and then on Mary Catherine, but their faces slid on by. I clutched the pew.

Across the aisle, Aunt Mariah stood up tall next to Papa, her eyes all fire and steel. *She is a soldier. A soldier about to kill her some Yankees.*

The organ music stopped.

"Please be seated," Reverend Evans said, his words squashed flat under the hum in my head. He opened up his Bible, and I held tight to his face with my eyes. "This morning's scripture reading comes from the book of Luke, the second chapter, verses one through sixteen." He cleared his throat. "'And it came to pass in those days, that there went out a decree from Caesar Augustus . . .'"

I tried to push away thoughts of sleeping soldiers and little rat bodies gone to mush with poison, but they kept coming. My stomach clenched. What would we do when we went back to a tavern room full of dead Yankees? What then?

"'. . . unto the city of David, which is called Bethlehem . . .'"

While I watched Reverend Evans's lips move, a queer feeling came to me, a prickle at the back of my neck. The Reverend favored Dempsey in the face, the Yankee feller who did not tattle on Will's thieving. The Reverend and Dempsey had the same way of looking away from folks they was talking to, and they had the same shape of chin. My heart thumped hard in my chest. *Dempsey was gone from Winfrey, though. He would not eat the biscuits.*

Ferdy used to say, "Breathe deep and slow," when I needed calming. I sucked in a chest full of air and blew it back out again, smooth as I could. At my side, Ferdy did the same, and I thought my heart might explode.

I shut my eyes and tried hard to take in only the Reverend's words. In the dark behind my eyelids, there was nothing to trick me into remembering the good in a Yankee.

"'And she brought forth her firstborn son . . .'"

Firstborn. Quick as that, Lieutenant Brandon was there in my head, saying, "We call him Robbie . . . firstborn and all that, you know." And then, "Feed the good wolf."

My eyes flew open. There was not just one decent Yankee, or two, but lots! I'd seen bad ones, but there was bad Confederates, too, and God would punish them all. I looked at Aunt Mariah across the aisle where she sat next to Papa, her chin stubborn, her hands clutching her Bible. Aunt Mariah was not God!

Reverend Evans's voice rose. "'A multitude of the heavenly host praising God, and saying, Glory to

God in the highest, and on earth peace, good will toward men.'"

I stood up, a lump closing up the space in my throat. I made the room steady in front of me.

"Lonzo, sit down," Papa said, quiet.

My heart beat faster. I could not sit down.

"Lonzo, sit down!" Papa said. The hard edge in his voice made me tremble, but I knew what I had to do. I did not care right then if Papa was proud of me or not.

"No, Papa, I can't," I said.

Papa's eyes opened wide as Aunt Mariah barked, "Lonzo, don't!"

But I turned and ran out of that church. I leaped down the marble steps and put on some speed, my lungs stinging with gulps of bitter cold air. Never mind the biting wind on my face or the icy patches trying to trip me up, I tore through town and then the Deep Cut, feeling the rail ties, rough through the holes in my boots. It didn't matter. Nothing mattered 'cept keeping the Yankees from eating them poisoned biscuits.

I got to the lane at Winfrey and saw soldiers crossing from their tents in the field up to Winfrey's front door. I rushed past them, knocking one off his feet and shoving another one aside.

"Hey!" I heard behind me. Somebody grabbed the back of my coat, but I wrenched away, hard.

I busted into the inn, blind at first in the dim-ness, and stumbled over something on the floor. A body! *Oh, please Lord, no!* My breath caught hard and sharp in my chest. *I was too late!*

Then, over the poundin' of my heart, I heard 'im groan. "Oww! Watch where you're goin', boy."

I jumped. He wasn't dead; only asleep!

I let out a breath, making my way fast as I could over and around the rest of the men on the floor. But when I got to where Aunt Mariah had left the plate of biscuits, they was gone!

I heard a chair scrape the kitchen floor, then a familiar rattling cough. *Grandpa!*

I burst through the door to see Grandpa lifting the towel off the plate in front of Grandma. "No!" I yelled, and grabbed the plate. At the back door I fumbled with the latch, then ran with the biscuits out into the yard, turning and turning, frantic for a place to get rid of them. I saw the well. *No, we got to drink that water.*

Then I saw the privy.

I ran, careful not to spill any of the biscuits off the plate, and snatched the door open quick. Thankful not to find some feller sitting there, I slung the biscuits off the plate and into that stinking hole. My breath caught in my throat and I stumbled back-ward onto the hard ground, shaking. My cheeks felt cold, and I wiped at 'em, surprised to find 'em wet with tears. How long had I been bawlin'?

Grandpa slapped the back door of the kitchen open and called, "Lonzo? Boy, where'd you go with them biscuits?"

I did not answer. I just sat, catching my breath, and choking back the sour taste of panic in my throat.

By and by Mr. Murphy's milk wagon rattled and clattered, reckless down the lane, and I heard Papa, who must've borrowed the wagon, yelling, "Whoa, whoa!" I went inside.

"What on God's green Earth *possessed* you, Mariah? *What possessed you?*" Papa hollered as he rushed in.

Aunt Mariah'd told him 'bout the poison?

Papa looked wild, his hair standing on end, and Aunt Mariah's face was all a'fury.

Grandpa started in again. "This boy swiped my biscuits right out from under my nose, Bernard! I finally get Miss Polly up them steps all on my own and what's he do? He steals our breakfast!"

Papa let out a gasp.

Aunt Mariah's face went white. "I fixed you a tray," she said. She turned to Papa. "I fixed them a tray . . ."

"Well, you left off the spoons," Grandpa said. "Can't eat cornmeal grits without spoons! I came upstairs to get us a couple. But when I got here and smelled them biscuits, I thought to myself: Wouldn't it be good for Miss Polly to eat fresh biscuits in a nice warm kitchen?"

There was a short spell of dead quiet.

Then a low moan came from Aunt Mariah, and she bent double, her head to her knees, before collapsing on the floor at Grandma's feet. "Oh, Mama," she sobbed. "I didn't mean them for you and Papa! I'm sorry, I'm sorry!"

Grandma, her eyes wide, looked at me, then at the empty plate on the table, then at Aunt Mariah. She tilted her head as a sharpness came to her eyes, and one hand flew to her mouth. "Lord have mercy," she whispered.

I heard the wind whistle around the corner of the house, then the *thump* of a piece of wood shifting in the stove. Grandma reached down and petted Aunt Mariah's hair. It'd come loose from under her hat, and Grandma smoothed it, tucking it back up again like Aunt Mariah was just a little girl.

Papa draped an arm around Grandpa's shoulder. "Papa," he said, soft, "did you or Mama eat any of the biscuits?"

"Would've if we'd had half a chance, Bernard," Grandpa said, *"but the boy threw 'em down the privy!"*

I thought he was going to go on about his breakfast bein' snatched again, but Papa pulled Grandpa close in a big hug, his shoulders shaking. Grandpa's amazed eyes peeked over Papa's shoulder, and he was quiet.

Nobody stirred.

By now, soldiers filled up the hallway and spilled

out into the kitchen, poking their heads 'round one another to see what was going on. One of them looked at me, then at the hairy feller next to him, and spoke up. "James," he said, nodding my way, "ain't he the slow one you was telling me about what danced?"

When I heard that, my stomach did not get sour or sick, and I didn't feel like screamin'. It did not matter a whit what that feller thought of me. I was fast enough to keep anybody from gettin' poisoned. I reckon that was exactly as fast as I needed to be.

Papa turned to the soldier. He looked at the feller's uniform and then into his bearded face. "Private, you best not be calling my son 'slow.'" His voice was strong and in-charge again.

I watched, amazed.

The whole room was still for a spell. Nobody moved, or talked; no new sounds came from any-where to chase Papa's words away.

Finally, Papa turned to me. I saw somethin' flash in the blue of his eyes, and he stared at me. "No, sir," he said. "My son is not slow."

Spring, 1864

After breaking winter camp, the troops had all moved away from Culpeper. They'd gone north to Pennsylvania and south to Georgia and west over the mountains and maybe east, too, spreading out from where we was like ripples on water, leaving us left behind in the calmness. There was no food left anywheres, but with the Yankees all gone, it was easier to tolerate an empty belly.

Lincoln had freed the slaves, too. Right away, Nellie and Lottie was gone, but Weezie'd stayed at Mama's and Papa's, probably on account of she didn't have family no place else. But old Samuel from Mr. Jameson's orchard, along with other Negroes from all around Culpeper, was gone, quick as a wink.

On my way to Papa's store for Aunt Mariah, I saw Mrs. Jameson, a proper lady like Mama, trying to hoe her trampled garden. When I told Papa, he said, "Well, I don't know what she's got to plant. I certainly don't have any seed to sell her. It's scarce as hens' teeth."

Aunt Mariah and me and Ferdy had dug up scatterlings ourselves the day before—tiny seedlings what had made it through all the terrors on their own, taking life in the warm soil after a dreadful cold winter. We planted them in new rows in the bright sunshine and watered 'em good. What would we eat till they grew big enough to bear vegetables?

"Now that the Yankees is gone, Papa, can I come home to live?" I asked. "I'm bigger and stronger now, and I'll work hard, I promise." It was not the work I loved to do, being inside that store, but I wanted to have my chance to please him again, now that I knew I could.

"Lonzo," he said, "what you're doing at Winfrey is more honorable."

"Honorable?" I asked. "How's it honorable?"

"You're taking care of people you love, son. I know you love your brothers and sisters, too, and your mother. But, well . . ."

I wanted to say then, *I love you, too, Papa*; but I didn't. Somehow, I knew it wasn't an easy thing for a man like Papa to hear.

He laid his hand on my arm and patted it like I was his friend. "Your Aunt Mariah and Ferdy need you more," he said. "And being around in that time of need, well, that's more honorable."

I remembered how Ferdy had talked of honor and glory before the war started. I reckoned honor must be like slowness, different things to different folks.

Me and Tish and Ferdy was on the road in front of Winfrey, Tish clasping Uncle Daniel's pocket watch in both her hands.

Faster! Pounding footsteps on the damp, packed dirt. Ragged breath. Sweat flying in the air.

"C'mon, *faster!*" Tish hollered. She jumped up and down behind the finish line I'd drawn in the dirt.

My heart pounded.

Tish looked up, and back at the watch again, her eyes getting bigger. Then, bounding to the side and out of the way, she let out a *whoop* and punched at the air. "Your best time ever!" she hollered.

"My—*best?*" Ferdy panted, pushing the words out of his mouth like they was stuck there, not wanting to budge.

Tish and me hugged, and grabbed Ferdy, dancin' him 'round in circles. He'd run straight as an arrow that time, not pitchin' side to side. He'd not dragged that leg while he walked, neither, for near on a month.

Once Ferdy got his first word out, I knew he would get better. Reverend Slaughter'd wound up givin' the books I'd rescued to Ferdy, and I'd been reading to him every day. One day, when I opened up a brand new book, I had trouble right off with the hard words on the first page. Ferdy'd waited for a spell, but then he grabbed *Oliver Twist* out of my hands. When I showed him the word, his eyebrows scrunched together and his mouth opened and closed, and then finally he shut his eyes, and out came, "Damn!" That wasn't the word on the page, and we stared at each other for a long second, finally bustin' out laughin' till there was tears in our eyes. When he got his breath back, he tried it again. "In-es-tim-able!" The word didn't mean nothing to me, except that Ferdy was coming back.

"You three going fishing or not?" Aunt Mariah called from the porch. "We're going to need some supper soon!"

"Yes, ma'am," I said, running to get the pail and our poles from where they leaned against the steps. "What else we having, Aunt Mariah?"

"Humph," Aunt Mariah said. "See if you can find some dandelion greens or poke on your way. I thought I had another jar of beets under the cellar steps, but they're gone. We must've eaten them already. Mercy, I'm forgetful! I'm getting more and more like Grandpa every day." She shook her head and went inside.

Ferdy let out a hoot. "Beets!" he said, grinning.

"You know something about them beets?" I said, watching Ferdy sideways and handing him his pole. We headed for Summerduck River, Ferdy still grinning.

"C'mon, Ferdy, tell us!" Tish said. "You didn't eat a whole jar of beets all by yourself, did you? That's shameful!"

Ferdy's eyes got big and he shook his head. "S- secret!" he said, serious.

"It's a secret?" Tish said. "Truly? You didn't eat them?"

"No," Ferdy said, the smile coming back.

We settled in on the bank at Summerduck. After the cold, gray winter, the green all around was a true miracle. I sat picking dandelion greens in a sunny spot while Ferdy and Tish dropped their lines in the water. Ferdy had balanced his on a log, like always. He found a stick nearby and peeled back its rough bark with his knife. Tish pulled Uncle Daniel's watch out of the deep pocket of her frock, then dropped it back in.

"What time you got to be back?" I asked her.

"Not for two hours," Tish said, her eyes on the water. "Sure are a mess more chores with Nellie gone. I'm glad they're freed up and all, but I miss her and Lottie."

"You getting on all right with your papa?" I asked,

piling the greens I'd gathered in a shady spot. I put my line in the water.

Tish bit her lip and lifted one of her bare feet to rub the other ankle. "We don't talk much," she said. "I think he's scared I'll tell him no to something again. I truly do."

I nodded, remembering how my head spun when I told my own Papa no in church at Christmastime. I didn't ever want to have that awful feeling again. Knowing I was not smart as Ferdy or Tish made it harder. I was bound to make a mistake. But sometimes, a wrong was so wrong, I flat-out forgot myself.

Ferdy scrambled to his feet, grabbing his pole, then pulled and backed up and pulled some more. Finally, out came a pretty trout. "Looky—*there!*" he said.

Tish caught one too, and Ferdy, two more; then Tish got another. My line dangled, still, in the water; but I did not mind. We'd have enough for supper.

Tish went home from the fishing hole, her hair swishing along her back, with two fish tied on a string. She was proud, I could see by how she carried 'em. I hoped Uncle Daniel would be, too.

The sun was startin' to lean to the west as we walked back to the inn. "Mama!" Ferdy hollered as we came across Winfrey's front yard. "Three fish!"

Aunt Mariah stepped out onto the porch, drying her hands on a towel. She smiled big at the pail I carried.

"Thank the Lord," she said. "Spring is surely here if the fish are biting. I was getting right tired of squirrel and rabbit." She turned to go inside.

"Mama?" Ferdy said again.

"What is it, Ferdy? I'm scrubbing the laundry."

Ferdy leaned his pole against the porch and dug in his pocket. He made a thinking face, eyes half-closed, giving his whole strength to the words in his head. "I've got a—present!" he said.

Aunt Mariah walked to the steps, leaving the towel over the rail, and sat down. "This isn't a frog, is it, son?" Her face was soft and teasing. "When you were little you brought me frogs; did you know that? I don't want a frog now, y'hear?"

Ferdy laughed, then stopped, shaking his head. "No frog," he said. He pulled his hand out of his pocket, slow.

First, all I saw was the silver chain Aunt Mariah used to wear around her neck, trailin' through Ferdy's fingers. My heart beat faster. Then, something red.

Aunt Mariah's hand went to her mouth.

I moved in closer, and Ferdy opened his hand. In it lay a small carved heart, perfect-shaped, one side to the other, worked near to smooth except for its little pointy bottom. A tiny groove ran round the edge, even as you please, and there was a little ring at the top where the chain went through.

"Oh, Ferdy," Aunt Mariah said, wiping tears off her cheeks with the back of her hand. "It's beautiful!"

"But—" Ferdy turned the carving over and pointed out a little cut just off from the center. "I slipped," he said, serious.

Aunt Mariah took the heart from Ferdy and clasped it to her chest. Then she held it out to marvel at it again. "Ferdy, it's perfect," she said, and sniffled. "It's just perfect."

She reached for Ferdy, pulling him to her in a big hug. Then suddenlike, she let him loose and studied the heart again. "How did you make it red?" she said.

Ferdy grinned. "Beet juice!" he said.

Me and Aunt Mariah laughed.

"Well, it's good to know I'm not losing my senses," she said. She lifted the chain over her head and settled the heart on the front of her dress, giving it a pat. Then she got to her feet and climbed the porch steps, taking up the towel she'd left on the rail. She stopped at the door to turn and chuckle at Ferdy again. "Beet juice!" she said, shaking her head, and went inside.

While Ferdy cleaned the fish out back, I went on with the work of springtime, gathering small branches what had fallen in the last windy storm, and turning clippings into the earth at the end of the garden. The air was sweet with a new-grass smell, and I smiled while I worked.

When I finished, I shoved my hands into my pockets and walked across the yard, breathing deep. The air was fresh and alive in my lungs and when I looked into the apple green leaves fluttering above my head, I almost felt like I could fly.

Under the black walnut tree, I looked up and tried to see the place where I hid my treasures so long ago. The Mexican penny and the arrowhead. And of course, Custard's fancy knife. But the place was hidden by the leaves. I grabbed a low branch and pulled myself up, climbing and climbing till I reached the spot.

I'd not been up there for months, and I had to look hard for the old knothole. Willowy branches, thin but strong like my new baby brother, Robert Lee, sprouted every which way. Finally I pushed aside a bunch, and there it was.

I could not see the penny or arrowhead a'tall, and new, thicker bark grew over the rusty edges of the knife, swallowin' it, like the tree was tryin' to heal the wound. I remembered the night I hid the knife—the madness racin' through me—and how I wanted to hurt that Yankee feller.

I was better now, though; all of us was. A body couldn't live riled like that forever. We could only take in what happened and figure the best way to go on.

That bark growin' over the knife was just like Ferdy, healing, and like Aunt Mariah, findin' a way to be happy again. It was like Culpeper, too, gettin' back to normal.

But most of all, it was like Papa and me. If Papa saw me before as the weak part of his family, that had changed. After somethin' is broke and mended again, sometimes it's the mended part that's strongest and best, like worn-out clothes turnin' into quilts.

Maybe that would be us now, me and Papa.

Author's Note

What Really Happened at Winfrey

The first time I heard the account of Aunt Mariah's poisoned biscuits, I was only eight or nine years old. It was Thanksgiving or Christmas, one of those occasions when lots of Rossons gathered around the dinner table.

But it wasn't just a story; it was true. Mariah Rosson actually ran Winfrey, an inn at the crossroads south of Culpeper, during the Civil War. She put poison in a batch of biscuits there, intending to serve them to the occupying Yankee troops.

(Another episode in *The Deep Cut*—that of the meat-house contents having been dumped into the mud and the geese subsequently beheaded—derived from an actual event as well. However, the victim in that case was Mrs. William Mason Yowell.)

Mariah's plan for the biscuits backfired. *The Deep Cut* is my invention—a wishful ending to a tragic reality. My great-great-great grandparents accidentally ate the biscuits laced with poison and died, Polly on December 17, 1863, and William Larkin the next day, December 18, 1863. I don't know how Mariah coped with the horror of her mistake, as there is little mention in family writings of her postwar life. I hope she was able to forgive herself and find some joy in her remaining years. She died in July 1883, a year before Ferdy married.

Uncles Edmund and Jack (Andrew Jackson Rosson) were both killed at Fort Donelson. I found

The Rosson House at 1001 South East Street, which Bernard Rosson built for his wife, Elvira, circa 1860. The people on the porch are presumed to be members of Lonzo's family. Photographer unknown.

no record of Ferdy having fought in the war. Though possible, it is unlikely, as he was only thirteen or fourteen in 1861, the year the war began. (Birth records conflict.) Tish got her wish, and was buried in the slave cemetery.

Alonzo James Rosson was just eight years old in 1861. He was listed in census records as an "invalid," common terminology at the time for describing the mildly retarded. I have often wondered if, had he been old enough in real life, he might have acted as heroically as his namesake character, Lonzo, did in *The Deep Cut.* I like to think so.

Alonzo James Rosson's headstone, Fairview Cemetery, Culpeper. Photo credit: John MacNair Rosson

The Deep Cut today, taken from the overpass.
Photo credit: John MacNair Rosson

ROSSON FAMILY TREE

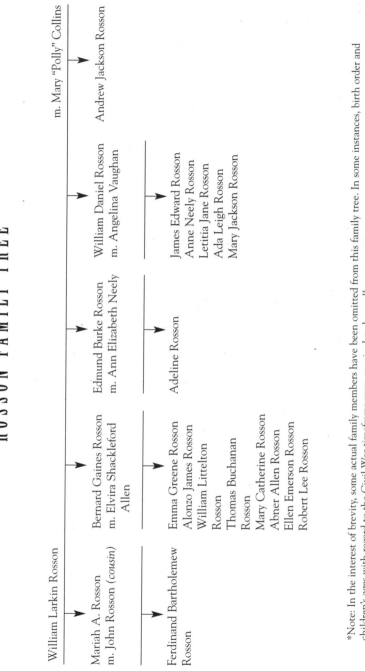

William Larkin Rosson — m. Mary "Polly" Collins

Mariah A. Rosson
m. John Rosson (*cousin*)

Bernard Gaines Rosson
m. Elvira Shackleford
Allen

Edmund Burke Rosson
m. Ann Elizabeth Neely

William Daniel Rosson
m. Angelina Vaughan

Andrew Jackson Rosson

Ferdinand Bartholemew
Rosson

Emma Greene Rosson
Alonzo James Rosson
William Littelton
Rosson
Thomas Buchanan
Rosson
Mary Catherine Rosson
Abner Allen Rosson
Ellen Emerson Rosson
Robert Lee Rosson

Adeline Rosson

James Edward Rosson
Anne Neely Rosson
Letitia Jane Rosson
Ada Leigh Rosson
Mary Jackson Rosson

*Note: In the interest of brevity, some actual family members have been omitted from this family tree. In some instances, birth order and children's ages with regard to the Civil War timeframe were manipulated as well.